"You're bea
grown-up

Quentin drew her to her feet and continued, "Why not forget the past and concentrate on me?"

Gasping at his audacity, Gina felt her heartbeats quicken. "Why the sudden change of heart?" she asked coolly. "You never noticed me before."

"You never used to look like you do now," he said huskily. "But I remember the few times I had you in my arms I didn't want to let you go. You must have known that."

"I remember you always pushed me away." Her eyes widened as she relived the hurt.

"I didn't want to frighten you. But you felt something, I'm certain."

"If I did," Gina lied, "I can't recall it."

"You need reminding?" Before she could escape, his mouth came down firmly over hers.

MARGARET PARGETER

the loving slave

Harlequin Books

TORONTO • LONDON • LOS ANGELES • AMSTERDAM
SYDNEY • HAMBURG • PARIS • STOCKHOLM • ATHENS • TOKYO

Harlequin Presents first edition August 1982
ISBN 0-373-10523-1

Original hardcover edition published in 1981
by Mills & Boon Limited

CHAPTER ONE

GINA, hearing the car coming before she saw it, took to her heels and ran all the way from the stables to the house, a distance of some two hundred yards. Her red hair streamed out behind her slender young body as she moved gracefully, like summer grass in the wind, but she cared nothing for any impression she might make. This was no time to remember that she was eighteen and grown up. Far more important that she catch Quentin before he entered the house. Matthews, the butler, never let her in there if he could help it, and she would rather talk to Quentin outside.

As his powerful car purred to a stop and he thrust open the door, she was there, grabbing his arm as he got out, terrified he might get away before hearing what she had to say.

'Quentin!' she cried breathlessly, her huge green eyes fixed anxiously on his hard, handsome face, 'I think there's something the matter with Hector.'

'Hector?' Quentin Hurst paused impatiently, frowning down at the young girl who was clinging to his arm like a limpet. He was tall and by comparison she was small. He towered above her, his frown deepening as his glance flickered over her hands. Her thin hands were shapely enough but less than clean, and she smelled of the stables. Already there was a grubby mark on the sleeve of his suit and, while he never jibbed at their cost, his suits were extremely expensive.

He had passed an exceptionally busy day and was tired, the board meeting that afternoon having proved particularly irksome. He didn't like to think he had a flock of fools for directors, but sometimes he was almost convinced of it. They relied too much on his brilliant judgment and, today, instead of bringing a perverse satisfaction, it had irritated more than usual. On top of this he had guests coming to dinner and could well have done without Gina and her troubles. Angrily he chose to forget her age and that the horse she mentioned was his favourite. She was paid, wasn't she, to deal with mishaps at the stables? It was high time she lost the childish habit of running to him every time something went wrong.

His glance moved over her coldly, condemnation in his eyes. 'Haven't I told you,' he said curtly, 'to send for the vet when you're in any doubt about anything? Damn it all, Gina, I'm not exactly a pauper and Richard has sufficient faith in your judgment to know you wouldn't bring him out unnecessarily.'

Stricken, Gina retreated in bewilderment, as Quentin removed her offending hands, dropping them back to her sides. 'I'm sorry,' she murmured uncertainly, unhappy at his obvious disapproval. Her eyes darkened with concentration on the harsh lines of his face. Perhaps she should have remembered he would be tired, but over the years she had often hung on his arm and he had never objected before. This was the first time he had looked at her with actual distaste.

'I'm sorry, Quentin,' she watched him intently, unconsciously seeking to hold him with entreating eyes. 'I thought I ought to ask your permission this time before sending for Richard.'

'You know if there's anything wrong . . .'

'Yes, but you did complain about the size of his bills.'

'Not his accounts so much as the number of visits, which I'm sure you'll agree is not quite the same thing. I only keep four horses.'

Stiffly, Gina retorted, 'He doesn't charge for all his visits, I'm sure.'

'Why not?'

Not caring for Quentin's terseness, she gazed at him

uneasily. Richard Hedley was a friend, one of the few she had, and she didn't want to say anything that might hurt him. 'He often looks in when he's passing, just to see that everything's all right.'

'If you were any other girl I might say in the hope of a romp in the hay, but not with you. This is what puzzles me.'

Gina was young and still innocent yet she could recognise an insult as well as anyone. Her smooth face flushed painfully. 'You don't think I'm pretty enough to warrant a—a romp in the hay, Quentin?'

'No,' he was as indifferently frank as the dark glance he cast over her. 'You're too young and too plain, besides never being any too clean.'

That was unfair, but she made no protest. She had looked on Quentin for so long as a kind of superior brother that she had learnt to accept his frankness without complaint.

She was startled when his hand shot out to grip her narrow shoulder, as though for a moment he would like to have shaken her. 'Don't you ever wash?' he snapped.

'I have a bath night and morning,' she replied mildly, 'whatever the weather.'

If he frowned over her rather peculiar wording, he dismissed it as irrelevant. 'Then I can't understand why you never look clean. Always half the stables on your face!'

This time his tone was hard enough to make her shrink. Didn't he realise it was no easy task looking after four horses, as well as her father? And the horses Quentin expected to be immaculately groomed and ready, at almost a moment's notice, for the enjoyment of himself and his friends.

'When I take people riding,' he went on coldly, taking the opportunity to release some of the day's tension on Gina's hapless head, 'I expect my stable girl to look as presentable as the mounts I supply.'

'I'm sorry, Quentin,' she said humbly, immediately

frightened he might send her away, 'I'll try to do better. I'm sorry to have bothered you about Hector, but I couldn't decide . . .'

'I think you could,' he interrupted abruptly, having started on her untidy appearance now apparently ready to find fault with everything about her. His eyes glinted on her long tumbled hair, her patched shirt, her ragged jeans, and his steely fingers dug painfully in her shoulder. 'You were after some attention yourself, I suppose?' he suggested sarcastically. 'I know I haven't been near the stables recently, Gina, but I have been busy. You can cope, can't you?'

Mutely Gina nodded, accepting this, for in part it was true, but she would never pretend about the horses. It hurt that Quentin should think she would. 'I'd better get back,' she said dully, twisting away from him.

'Gina!' his command was sharp, swinging her around. 'What do you think is wrong with Hector?'

Too anxious about the horse to feel offended for long, she hesitated before replying. 'I'm not sure. He's been sweating a lot. It could be colic, but there are other things. Since I noticed something was wrong I haven't given him any food or water.'

'Send for Richard,' Quentin advised briefly, his hard features a little kinder. 'I mustn't forget how my father used to swear by this intuition of yours. He often said it was infallible.'

'Thank you, Quentin.' She would rather he had praised her expertise or common sense, but perhaps intuition was part of it. She smiled at him, her tired face suddenly lighting up. 'I'll ring Richard at once.'

At the stables she did just this, and was fortunate enough to catch Richard in. He promised to be with her within the hour. Like Quentin's late father, he too had a great respect for her judgment, when it came to horses.

After speaking to him, Gina saw it was well after six. If she hurried she might just have time to pop home and see

John. If he was in a good mood she might be able to
persuade him to eat some supper.

Hector, Quentin's thoroughbred hunter, was standing
in his loosebox exactly as she had left him. Why wasn't he
making a fuss, demanding her attention, being as autocratic as his master? Usually, when he knew she was near,
if Hector didn't turn his head he tossed it, just to let her
know he considered himself vastly superior to the soft-
voiced young girl who attended him.

'I'll not be long, old boy,' gently she rubbed her hand
along his proud neck, feeling that he was still hot. Sadly
she wished Mr Hurst had still been alive. Between the
two of them they had been able to solve most things.
Everything she knew about horses he had taught her,
until she had become almost as expert as himself. With
her quick intelligence she had never needed to be told
anything twice, but she missed their lengthy discussions,
his ready advice. Quentin loved horses, too, but he spent
most of his days in London, which wasn't quite the same,
although she tried to be fair. Quentin, at thirty-five, had
a business to run, whereas his father had been retired.

Gina lived in a cottage in the middle of the thick
woods which lay at the back of the main house and
grounds. The other land on the estate, or most of it, was
rented out, but Mr Hurst had insisted on keeping the
woods exactly as they were, because of the wild life which
he had studied with ever-increasing interest during the
last years of his life. Gina worried that one day soon
Quentin would wake up to their rampant disorder and
start on them. Quentin was an entirely different proposi-
tion from his father, there being little softness in his make-
up. And, although he enjoyed riding and living in the
country, she suspected his ruling passion was high fi-
nance. Young as he was, he was rapidly gaining a formid-
able reputation for it. He also had a reputation for being
extremely ruthless when it came to getting his own way,
whether in business or pleasure. Eventually, when he

came to deal with the dark, overgrown woods, Gina feared they might get the same kind of treatment.

The cottage, damp from the drip of overhanging branches and leaking spouts, seemed to watch her approach with an oddly gloomy expression. Pushing open the creaking door, she reminded herself that she must remember to oil the hinges. They were very rusty, but a little oil might help. There was no sign of her father. As she hurried over the bare flagged floor of the kitchen to his bedroom, her heart felt heavy as she saw he wouldn't want any supper this evening. The monthly sum he received from a private source he would never disclose must have arrived, and somehow he had managed to get hold of some whisky again. Bleakly she gazed at him as he lay in a drunken sleep. His heart was extremely bad, yet he kept on drinking heavily, slowly killing himself.

Gently, her heart aching for him, she replaced the fallen rugs around his unconscious body. Then she left him, quietly closing the door. It was difficult to believe that John, as he always insisted his daughter call him, had once been a well known and successful surgeon. Gina doubted if anyone, seeing him now, would believe it. She had felt completely incredulous, herself, when she had first learnt this from Quentin's father just a week or two before he died, especially as that was all he would divulge. When, in shocked surprise, she had asked Mr Hurst why he had told her this, he had replied, grim-faced, that it had something to do with his conscience. It was something, he insisted, she should have been told long ago, but if she wished to know more then she must go to John himself.

John had flown into what was, for him, quite a rage when confronted, and would tell her little more than she had learnt from Mr Hurst. The loss of his wife, Gina's mother, through a mistake which had cost a life, had resulted in him giving up his career and coming to live here. Once he had done Andrew Hurst a good turn and, in return, Andrew had given him a quiet old cottage to live in. Quentin, he said, had never known him, nor had Andrew's wife. They both thought John was a casual acquaintance whom Andrew had taken pity on. Neither of them, so far as Gina was aware, had ever visited the cottage.

Gina stopped asking questions only when it became quite clear that John wasn't going to answer them. Gradually she learnt to accept her father's explanations, brief though they were, and to forget. There seemed nothing else she could do. Time passed and she left school, after Andrew Hurst died. He had always been kind to her and she mourned him. She certainly never felt he owed her anything. Whenever she thought of him now it was always with gratitude that he had been a friend, and had taught her so much about horses and stable management.

Before leaving she threw some more logs on the fire. They were damp as she had only sawn them this morning. Andrew had allowed them to collect the fallen wood around the cottage and she still did so, hoping that if Quentin found out he wouldn't raise any objections. Fortunately he never came near, keeping to the open fields when he was out riding, and too engrossed with his business in London to give the woods or what was in them a second thought.

Richard Hedley was there when she returned to the stables, but he had just arrived. 'Hello, Gina,' he smiled at her. 'What seems to be the trouble?'

'I'm not sure, maybe nothing much,' she said more or less the same to him as she had said to Quentin. 'It's Hector . . .'

'Ah, his lordship's favourite!'

Gina bit her lip. 'You shouldn't call Quentin that, Richard. After all, he isn't a lord.'

'He can act like one!'

'Maybe sometimes,' she admitted, 'but not always. He can be very nice.'

'When it suits him.'

Glancing at Richard wryly, Gina wondered why there should be so much antagonism between two men who had apparently known each other all their lives. 'You'd better have a look at Hector,' she tried to change the subject tactfully. 'I'm very worried about him.'

'Right!' Richard immediately reverted to what he was for the greater part of each day and often during the night, a very competent veterinary surgeon. Together they went into the stables.

Before entering Hector's loosebox, Richard spoke to him quietly. Hector knew the vet and liked him and stood quite still.

'Has Quentin seen him yet?' Straightening from his examination of the big horse, Richard glanced at the anxious girl by his side.

'No—not yet. He has guests coming, this evening, but he did say he would look in later if he has time. What is it, Richard?'

Richard grimaced. 'I think he's been gorging himself on too rich a pasture. At a guess.'

Gina frowned. 'I had a horrible feeling it might be my fault,' she confessed unhappily. 'You see, I didn't have time to exercise him long enough myself, so I let him graze in the river field.'

'You mean he's too strong for you?'

She didn't answer this, not directly, having a weary suspicion it might be true. 'My father wasn't well yesterday, Richard. That was why I was so pushed for time, but I feel dreadful about Hector,' she put a hand remorsefully on his silky coat. 'It's all my fault.'

'Never mind,' Richard wouldn't allow this, 'we can all make mistakes. You did the right thing in sending for me, though. When a horse is valuable it doesn't pay to take risks.'

'It's the horse that's important, surely, not his value?'

Gina raised a small, indignant face.

'Of course, you're quite right,' Richard soothed, 'but Quentin mightn't think so.'

This frightened Gina. 'No, he might not,' she agreed soberly. 'Hector cost a great deal of money.'

'Well, we'll soon have him fit again.' Richard, sensing her alarm, was reassuring. 'There's not much damage done. Nothing that can't be cured with a little extra care and attention.'

'Oh, I'm so glad!' Gina's face, suddenly radiant with relief, caught Richard unawares. He stared at her, as if only beginning to realise that under her untidy appearance lay a beautiful girl. He blinked, unable to look away. He was a male of thirty, his sole passion animals, but now he had a strange feeling that this was about to change.

Gina noticed with perplexity his rather dazed expression. 'Richard, what is it?'

'Gina,' he exclaimed, 'how old are you?'

'Eighteen,' she smiled, trying not to feel uneasy. 'I left school almost a year ago.'

'Are you going on to university?'

She had a feeling that Richard was just talking for talking's sake, and shook her head. 'No, I hardly think so. I enjoy looking after Quentin's horses.'

'But that would be a waste.'

'It depends——' she shrugged.

'On what, for heaven's sake?'

'Why,' she was startled that he was so intense, 'I suppose on what one wants from life. University doesn't appeal to me.'

'I can't think why this should.' Tersely his glance roamed the shadowed stables before returning to rest enquiringly on Gina's face.

Gina merely smiled, her wide, innocent smile which entranced unconsciously. The man watching her unexpectedly caught his breath, but before he could add anything further, she said anxiously, 'Perhaps we should talk about Hector?'

Pulling himself quickly together, Richard obliged. He was a good vet and didn't often allow himself to be diverted from a sick animal, not even by someone as suddenly interesting as Gina.

Later, as he was leaving, she said, 'I'll pass what you've told me on to Quentin. I'm sure he'll look in, after his guests have gone.'

'You can't wait here?'

'Why not? It wouldn't be the first time, and I've things to do.'

'You could wait a long time,' he warned gruffly. 'Some of Quentin's guests are pretty potent, from what I've seen.'

Vaguely Gina thought of this as she completed her tasks for the day. Already Hector seemed easier and she had every confidence in Richard. It was Quentin she was unsure of. In spite of his apparent indifference and his sophisticated girl-friends, she knew he would be worried about Hector. She didn't want him arriving here and then coming on to the cottage, looking for her. He was unpredictable and he just might, and she would rather he didn't come anywhere near the cottage.

Her work completed, she sat down on a bale of straw, still undecided what to do. Earlier, at the house, Quentin had called after her that he would look in later and, for all Richard had hinted otherwise, he always kept his word. Wearily she frowned, leaning back on the straw, feeling drowsy, but she didn't remember falling asleep.

Her dreams were disturbed and she moaned softly, then opened her eyes to find Quentin shaking her roughly, as if her sleep had been deeper than she thought.

'Gina, wake up!' he was saying curtly. 'Are you all right? You shouldn't be here at this time of night.'

'Quentin?' she murmured, confused by sleep, blinking up at him.

'Come on, Gina, pull yourself together!'

The impatience in his voice, getting through to her at last, hurt, though she was used to it. Unexpectedly, for she never wept if she could help it, her eyes filled with tears. 'I waited for you,' she whispered, 'to tell you about Hector.'

'You needn't have. Richard rang. He told me all I need to know.'

That didn't sound good. Alarm flitted through her, but because he crouched over her she was unable to move. The eyes she raised to his were wide and drenched with tears, remarkably beautiful, as was the full curve of her trembling mouth with its short, endearingly childish upper lip.

Whether Quentin was moved by her tears or something else, she never knew, but his voice softened. 'Don't cry, Gina girl. It's not important.'

She tried to speak, but her voice choked and she was unable to continue. Her tears flowed faster and she put a hand to her eyes. It was a childish gesture and it seemed to be his undoing. With a gentle murmur he pulled her into his arms and began stroking her hair.

'Gina . . .' Suddenly he bent his head and kissed her, lightly and affectionately, his mouth just touching hers, yet there was a very pleasurable sensation. Frowning, he drew back, his eyes on her face. Gina heard his breathing roughen, but was barely conscious of it, as something was affecting her, too.

Another tear slid down her hot cheek, leaving a mark. Quentin frowned, his own momentary surprise forgotten in the face of her continuing distress. 'Don't,' he muttered, drawing her closer, instinctively protective.

The feeling was there again. As her slight body clung to his it was there, spreading through them, a fire, one which threatened to burn. Abruptly, as if regretting his former impulse, he put her from him.

'I'll see you home, Gina.' He didn't look at her. 'You're upset about Hector, but he'll be much better tomorrow, you'll see.'

'Yes, of course.' Gina, wide awake now, jumped to her feet. Her limbs seemed stricken by a curious weakness and she wondered why. Clumsily she stumbled. 'I can see myself home, Quentin. There's no need for you to come.'

'Did you have a coat?' He was viewing her thin shirt doubtfully.

'No,' she gave Hector a last caress, happy to see the big horse was taking some notice of her again. 'It's not raining, is it?'

'No,' Quentin closed the stable door, 'but it's cold.'

'Goodnight,' she smiled at him briefly through the darkness.

'I said, Gina, I would see you home.'

Her heart sank. When Quentin spoke like that she never argued. He had changed, she noticed, into jeans and a black sweater—she couldn't even suggest he would ruin his clothes. Oh, well, it was dark. With any luck the darkness would hide what she didn't want him to see, and he wouldn't come farther than the door. Men like Quentin never stepped inside tumbledown cottages, and he would be in a hurry to get back to his guests.

So she deluded herself. The path through the woods was rough, but it was Quentin who stumbled, not Gina. She heard the terse expletives he rasped under his breath. She wanted to tell him there wasn't really room to walk two abreast, but a certain dread she could put no name to kept her silent. She had a terrible feeling that something dreadful was about to happen.

At the cottage she halted. 'I can manage now, Quentin.' For the first time since he had kissed her she met his eyes. 'Your—guests will be wondering what's become of you.'

'Let them,' he replied brusquely. 'I'll see you inside. There's no light?'

Stubbornly she didn't move. 'My father will be in bed. It—it might disturb him if he hears voices.'

'I'd have thought he would be more disturbed not to,' he rejoined cryptically. 'If I had a child like you I'd be as worried as hell if I thought you were wandering in woods like these at this time of night.'

'He knows I'm used to them,' she protested feebly. 'I know them like the back of my hand.'

'I'm not impressed.' He grabbed her arm grimly. 'Are you going to ask me in or do we skip the invitation?'

It wouldn't matter whether she invited him or not. He meant to be inside, she could tell. Bitterly she wondered why he bothered asking. Reluctantly she opened the door.

'Where's the damned light?' Quentin let go of her arm to grope on the wall for the switch instead of following her down the passage. As she halted abruptly, he came after her, nearly tripping over her in the darkness. Again she flinched, as their bodies collided, and a peculiar feeling shot through her. 'We aren't on the mains,' she said.

'Not on the mains!'

The logs she had placed on the fire earlier gave off a faint glow and she could see him looming furiously over her, his tall, lean-hipped elegance seeming quite out of place in such shabby surroundings. With shaking hands she pushed at her untidy hair. 'We have lamps and candles.'

'Light something, then.' His voice was alive with suppressed violence.

She didn't want to, she wished he would leave. 'I think I'll go straight to bed, without a light,' she muttered.

'Gina! Do as I say—and at once!'

Finding the matches, she lit a candle, which was all there was until she could afford some more oil for the lamp. The solitary candle, stuck crookedly in the middle of a jam jar, flared into life and she stared at Quentin defiantly.

He wasn't looking at her. His eyes were travelling swiftly around, noting the bare stone floor, the uncurtained window, the scratched, uneven surface of the table. At last he spoke. She considered he took his time. 'Where do you cook, Gina, if you have no electricity?'

'I don't cook much, but there's the fire.'

He merely glanced at the rusty, old-fashioned range which was clearly too old to function. 'Do you have a tap?'

For a moment she was bewildered. 'Oh, you mean water?' she nodded eagerly. 'Yes, we have a pump at the door.'

'A pump at the door! I see,' he said grimly. 'No wonder you never look clean.'

Flinching from the hardness of his voice, she retorted sharply, 'Sometimes I swim in the lake.'

She didn't feel the least embarrassed about Quentin knowing, if he had to. He saw her merely as a nuisance of a child, and, while he often blew his top at her, she seldom remembered his anger. The lake covered five acres and was private. Few people were aware of its existence and fewer still ever went there. She supposed because it was dark and deep, enclosed by the same woods that surrounded the cottage, on the edge of some wild heathland.

'How do you manage in winter?'

She wished he would stop speaking so tersely. 'I swim all the year round,' which was true, and meant she couldn't possibly not be clean! 'I never feel the cold.'

'And your father?'

She had to smile at the thought of her father bathing in the lake, although he once told her he'd been a good swimmer. 'I believe he makes do with the pump, at the door.' Her smile widened, in innocent amusement.

Her smile seemed to do it. She seemed to feel, before

she saw it, Quentin's sudden explosion of fury. 'It's no laughing matter, Gina!' He took hold of her, shaking her as he spoke, until sparks from his hands began hitting her unmercifully. 'It won't do,' he snapped. 'It won't do at all!'

'Let me go, Quentin!' she cried.

As if becoming aware of what he was doing, he stopped as abruptly as he had begun, and stood watching her, a brooding look on his face as she rubbed her sore arms.

Illogically, she gasped, 'I don't know about having no electricity, but when you touch me I can feel it all over.'

A flicker of wariness darkened his eyes and was gone. 'You deserve more than a shaking,' he rebuked her. 'Living like this and not mentioning it!'

'Who would I mention it to?' she asked quietly, suddenly afraid.

For an instant he appeared nonplussed. The silence lengthened, then he said curtly, 'I realise I should have known about the condition of my own property; but I haven't been in these woods for years. My father and I didn't see eye to eye about them. I wanted them cleaned up. Not cut down,' he insisted tersely, as Gina's eyes widened, 'but you know he wouldn't hear of them being touched. God knows,' he ran an impatient hand over his thick dark hair, 'I've had problems enough over the past ten years, getting the business back on its feet. Persuading my father to retire and hand over the reins was a major operation. I had to humour him regarding the woods. It seemed the only way.'

'He loved them,' Gina smiled softly, recalling the old man's delight.

Quentin nodded shortly.

Secretly she studied him, from under thick, curling lashes, as he turned to pace around the kitchen. She was well aware that Quentin Hurst was a wealthy man, but that he had worked for every penny he had made. The grey at his temples vouched for this, and while it added to

his air of distinction it wasn't usual in a man of his age.
He worked like a slave, and it was rumoured he was fast
reaping his rewards, but it had left its mark. Gone was
the relaxed, more tolerant younger man Gina had known
as a child, and in his place was a hard, successful tycoon,
a business magnate with much less heart. He took what
he wanted and was clever enough to get away with it.

Confused, Gina continued to stare at him, not able to
decide why this was becoming so clear to her now. Why
she should suddenly be seeing him, not through the eyes
of a child, or even a young girl, but as a woman. And
while she wasn't any too sure she liked what she saw,
there was something about him that drew her like a moth
to a flame. The shiver of cold premonition which went
through her was visible as he halted beside her and
looked at her quickly.

'You've left school, I take it?'

'Yes. A year ago.'

His glance sharpened. 'How old are you?'

'Eighteen.' He was the second person to ask within
hours. She couldn't think why.

'You don't look it.' The sneer on his lips was far from
flattering.

'Well, I am.' She stared sullenly back at him.

'Untidy, given to sulks, scarcely fit to be seen. And you
wonder why I doubt you're anywhere near eighteen?' His
tongue berated her harshly, without mercy. 'What are
you going to do with yourself?'

Why should Richard and he both be curious about
that? Richard's query had been kinder, though. He
didn't despise her as Quentin did. 'I don't want a career,'
she replied hesitantly, 'if that's what you mean.'

'It is.'

'I look after your horses,' she reminded him, 'and my
father couldn't do without me.'

'Wait a minute!' He paused, something obviously just
occurring to him. 'What are you paid? Come to that, who

pays you? I don't recall seeing your name on the books, which I occasionally check.'

'I work for the rent of the cottage,' she improvised quickly, feeling herself go cold again. Quentin's question, though she had been half expecting it for some time, had given her a shock. It was true his father had let them live here rent-free, but when she began helping in the stables he had given her a small wage as well. This had proved extremely welcome as John usually drank most of the allowance he received. Unfortunately when Mr Hurst died her wages had stopped. Of course Quentin couldn't be expected to know this, and she had known, if she told him, he would only say a free cottage was more than enough. If she complained it would provide him with an excuse to throw them out, and she could think of nothing worse than having nowhere to live. Even so, the last few months had been hard; she had often been both cold and hungry.

'I'm going to have a word with your father,' Quentin said coldly. 'Make yourself something to eat while I'm talking to him. Have you had any dinner?'

'I'm not hungry,' her appetite had left her, 'and John will be asleep.'

'Then perhaps it's time he woke up!' Quentin replied enigmatically.

'You don't understand!' Gina protested anxiously.

'I mean to,' he returned, in the same threatening tones, as he went through the door.

Gina knew what he would find but was helpless. Nothing would stop Quentin from crossing the narrow passage to find John. Despairingly she hoped he would find John's bedroom first. It was nothing special, but it did have a carpet of sorts on the floor, while hers had nothing but bare boards.

Minutes later Quentin was back, a tight anger on his lean face, that she didn't like. Unwittingly she shrank from him.

'How long has your father been like this?' he asked curtly.

She didn't pretend not to understand. 'As long as I can remember,' she answered him miserably, yet with a curious stoicism. 'He's been worse lately. His health is bad.'

'No wonder!' Quentin's voice was clipped, his eyes dangerously dark.

'You don't understand,' she cried, looking away from him.

'Gina!' his harsh grasp on her shoulders conveyed his contempt without words. 'It doesn't take a genius to understand what's going on here. Your father is an alcoholic.'

CHAPTER TWO

'YOUR father is an alcoholic,' Quentin said again.

'He can't be!' she whispered.

'A bad case, I should say.' He didn't spare her.

'And I'm not clean . . .'

His mouth tightened at the wild tears in her eyes. 'You've obviously not been properly brought up.'

Gina bit her lip painfully. He could be right, but for her father's sake she had to protest. 'I'm sure it's not that. Sometimes soap is expensive.'

'You'd be better off in a home,' he exclaimed.

'I'm too old!' she cried, aghast that such a thing should even cross his mind. 'Quentin?' she beseeched him desperately. 'Just leave things as they are, please! You have enough to think of without worrying about me.'

He studied her, her thin young body, the tangled hair tied tightly back, the huge green eyes fixed on him in unwavering appeal. 'It isn't you I'm worrying about,' he said cruelly. 'I can't let you go on living here, because one of these days someone is going to start asking questions, and I might easily be fined for allowing anyone to live under such conditions. Why, it's no better than a hovel!'

'Who would start asking questions?'

'Richard sounded much too interested this evening when he rang, although I can't think why.'

Gina hung her head. 'I think he likes me because I like horses.'

'Possibly.' Quentin could understand this, she saw.

She wished she could have given him a drink. John would have enough in his room, but she shrank from that. It wasn't often she resented living the way they did, but for once she thought how nice it would have been to have been able to offer hospitality. If she had been able to offer Quentin something he might have overlooked a lot of the things that seemed to be annoying him so greatly.

A week ago she had hung around the big house, in the hope of seeing Quentin. As usual, she had wanted to speak to him about the horses. Eventually she had crept up to the drawing-room window, to try and catch his attention. The scene inside had held her immobile for several seconds. Quentin had been there with his mother and several guests, having pre-dinner drinks. The dresses and jewellery of the women had glittered impressively against the luxurious background. Quentin, tall and darkly attractive with his broad shoulders and hard, sensuous mouth, had been talking to a young and beautiful woman, Blanche Edgar. Gina immediately recognised her, as she often spent the weekend at Briarly and Quentin took her riding. Knowing it would be a waste of time trying to see him that evening, Gina had turned away. Blanche Edgar was sophisticated, amusing and rich, and she had all his attention.

'I can make you a cup of tea?' she suggested unhappily.

'I'm afraid you can't bribe me with that,' he refused dryly. 'I'll see you tomorrow some time, Gina. Meanwhile, I'll give the whole matter of you and your father—and the cottage—some serious thought.'

Something in his face alarmed her badly. 'I won't agree to leaving, Quentin, I'm warning you!' she stared at him defiantly.

A flush of anger on his cheeks, he turned to the door. 'Don't ever threaten me, my child. I mightn't be much of a friend, but fight me and I'll make sure you regret it. You'd find me much worse as an enemy.'

After Quentin left Gina was unable to settle. In the short time he had been here he had managed to make her feel extremely worried about the future, and conscious of the defects of the cottage in a way she had never been before. It was, she supposed, little more than a hovel, but it was the only home she could remember and in spite of what Quentin said, she was fond of it.

One of the things that strangely seemed to disturb her most was his belief that she didn't wash. In a cracked mirror, in the shabby little closet she called her bedroom, she peered at her face. Across her cheek was a grubby mark, there was another on her forehead, and her hair was dull and untidy. Unhappily she compared herself with Quentin's glamorous friends and thrust the mirror quickly back in the drawer. No wonder he had been so scornful!

Suddenly she knew she couldn't go to bed until she had got rid of all the dust Quentin so disapproved of. Tonight she was so tired she had meant to make do with the pump at the door, but the water that came out of that was often so discoloured it was impossible to wash properly. It would only take a few minutes to reach the lake, and, with the air turning suddenly warmer again, the thought of a cool dip was inviting. Something else occurred to her too; on her way back she could look in on Hector.

Her father still slept and she sighed over him as she ran outside. From long experience she knew he would sleep until morning. With a flicker of hope she wondered if Quentin might be able to do something for him. He might know exactly what should be done. But, if he did come up with something, would John co-operate? Gina feared he wouldn't, not when she counted the number of times she herself had tried to get him to see a doctor.

'I've forgotten more than the majority of them will ever know,' he would snap, which had never made sense to her until she had discovered from Mr Hurst that her father had once been a famous surgeon. Even then, it hadn't made proper sense, not when John hadn't prac-

tised for years. But none of Gina's persuasions could move
him. 'I don't want to get well,' he would snarl. 'What
does it matter if I die?'

Gina knew the woods so well she could find her way
through them quickly. The lake was barely a mile away,
the pale water gleamed invitingly, its coolness irresistible
to her heated flesh. Quickly she slipped out of her sticky
clothing, loving the softness of the air on her skin after the
roughness of her shirt.

Leaving her clothes carelessly where she dropped them,
she waded into the lake. From this point it was impossible to dive as the bottom of the lake hadn't been
cleaned out for years and the edges were choked with
weeds. Once clear of them she swam for about a hundred
yards towards the small island in the middle. It was then,
as she paused for a brief rest, that she noticed the atmosphere was growing strangely oppressive.

She was used to the darkness, the inky green shadows
in the depth of the lake, but this evening the silence
seemed suddenly eerie. It weighed down on her, making
her unusually nervous. In all the time she had been
coming here she had seen no one, but she had always
delighted in the isolation of the lake, considering it, after
a while, as her own private domain. Never, until now,
could she remember feeling apprehensive. The water was
cool, she usually found it invigorating, but tonight it appeared to be having quite the opposite effect. Admitting
she was a coward but unable to help it, she turned back
towards the shore. A moment later she knew she had
done the right thing in following her instincts when the
skies were suddenly split open by a vivid flash of lightning.

A storm! She had never been here during a storm
before. At the cottage when a storm came it was frightening, with the huge trees outside making a great din and
the old roof rattling. Yet here in the middle of the lake it

was much worse. Fear lending strength to her slender limbs she swam quickly, while about her the flashes of lightning and rumbles of thunder increased as the centre of the storm drew nearer. The sky was lit up and forks of electricity seemed to dance over the water, reflecting in and emphasising the dark depth below her, making her conscious of her own danger.

She was near the edge of the lake when the tree was struck. It was one of the massive oaks which had probably stood there for hundreds of years, and it came down with a crash and painful creaking of protesting timber which almost deafened her. It was terrifying, she saw it coming but was unable to escape. Dazed, she heard herself screaming while trying to dive out of its path, convinced her last moment had arrived. Losing control for a moment, she screamed again, half blinded with terror, and didn't see the man cutting through the water with swift, powerful strokes towards her.

Miraculously neither the trunk of the tree nor any of its branches touched her, but the waves from it completely engulfed her, almost drowning her as they swept her under. Spluttering wildly, she tried to fight the black, churning waters, but they were too much for her. Then, as though the nightmare was continuing, she felt arms going round her, arms which her fevered mind assured her must belong to the spirit of this devilish night as they tightened ruthlessly about her and refused to let her go.

It took her some seconds to realise that the voice she heard shouting in her ear was Quentin's. The Devil, surprisingly, was nowhere to be seen, unless it was in the black glitter of Quentin's eyes.

'Stop struggling, Gina, or I'll hit you!'

His voice was harsh, almost as harsh as his breathing and instinctively she obeyed him. Somehow she knew if she didn't she would drown. She was trembling, unable to stand, as he swam with her to the shore and lifted her bodily from the water. Clinging to him, she choked help-lessly against the hard wetness of his chest as he strode up the bank away from the lake and laid her on the grass.

'Have you swallowed much water, Gina?'

She was quite conscious, if she couldn't yet find the strength to sit up. 'No, I don't think so,' she managed to answer after clearing her throat a little. She felt more drowned outside than in, and strangely exhausted.

He brushed back her streaming hair with angry fingers. 'You little fool! What made you come here at this time of night, and in such weather?'

'It was quite fine when I set out,' she gasped. 'I always come for a swim.'

'You can thank God I remembered,' he said savagely, reaching for his discarded sweater to dry some of the water from her.

Not understanding, she asked weakly, 'What do you mean by that?'

Briefly he replied, 'It came back to me suddenly, what you said about having a bath, night and morning. It seemed crazy to think of the lake, but I decided to take a look. You could have been drowned, you little fool! Couldn't you see the storm coming?'

He sounded as savage as his hands were, bringing life back to her numbed body. It was the second time he had called her a fool, but she certainly deserved it. 'I'm sorry,' she whispered humbly, straining to see his face through the darkness, 'I won't do it again.'

'You'd better not!' His voice roughened, as he recalled moments of horror he would rather forget. 'When I saw that tree coming down and your head in the water . . .!'

'I'm sorry,' she repeated abjectedly, as another flash of lightning lit the scene brightly. It was only for a second, but enough to remind her that she was naked, and that Quentin wore merely a pair of briefs. Obviously he must have ripped off his clothes before diving into the lake, and now he was using his sweater to dry her.

'My jeans?' she spluttered, going hot all over. She felt terribly embarrassed and Quentin must be despising her—even more than usual. Apprehensive and shocked, she huddled away from him.

'Stop it, Gina!' He jerked her back, as if frightened of losing her again in the darkness. Indifferently taunting, he informed her, 'You aren't the first woman I've seen without her clothes, and it's not always an improvement, but in your case I think it might be. In fact I'm sure of it.'

This only confirmed her suspicions that he was viewing her with his usual contempt, and she shivered, confused by the sudden heat in her body.

'You're shaking, Gina. Have you any idea where your clothes are?'

'Where they always are,' she frowned, 'but I don't seem to know where I am.'

'That's understandable.' His crisp dark head was thrown up and he sounded terse. 'My sweater's damp now, but you'd better wear it. It's better than nothing.'

He was concerned for her and she was filled with remorse. He must have risked his life to save her and she hadn't even said thank you! She would hate him to think she didn't care.

'Quentin——' As he lifted his sweater to slip it over her head, she reached up simultaneously to press a brief, grateful kiss on his cheek. It was an impulsive gesture, prompted partly by a mind too disturbed by the experience she had just been through to fully realise what she was doing. As she reached up, with her chaste, appreciative kiss, their arms collided in mid-air, and, as his head jerked down, instead of finding his cheek, her lips touched his mouth.

Startled by this, she would have drawn back. If she hadn't there was no doubt Quentin would, for she heard his breath rasp impatently. But suddenly it was there between them again—the swift, melting sweetness, the sear

of fire, a surge of desire that made the senses spin. Swiftly
it rendered her helpless to move, for she didn't know how
to combat it.

Quentin must have known, but, as if he chose not to,
his breathing changed as her mouth moved convulsively
under his, and the sweater fell from his hands as he slid
them down her back to pull her closer.

'Gina?' he muttered thickly.

'I was trying to thank you,' she murmured, her voice
scarcely audible. She felt drugged, in no way alarmed by
the tightening pressure of his arms. She felt, in some
peculiar way, part of him.

If she had tried to fight him he might have let her go,
but her clinging arms appeared to urge him on. Quentin
Hurst was thirty-five and while unmarried had never
been particularly celibate, but when he was with a
woman, in similar circumstances, it was always by
mutual agreement. This evening there was no sophisticated, unemotional arrangement, but, as though suddenly possessed of the devil Gina had suspected in the
lake, he pushed her back against the bank and began
kissing her.

The weight of his body was heavy on hers, his mouth
urgent, demanding her response, impatiently seeking that
which she was apparently so eager to give. If she had
been drowning in the lake it was worse now, with Quentin sweeping aside all her token resistance, as though he
meant wholly to possess her. Between them reared a primitive, almost frightening sensuality, a wild flaring of the
senses, born perhaps of the wildness of the night, but all
the more devastating for that. The feeling between them
seemed to mount amazingly. They might have been twin
souls, succoured by the fierceness of the elements, well
able to destroy each other, although neither was yet
aware of it.

Their vivid, unexpected response to each other, heat-

ing as it did the coldness of their bodies, seemed in step
with the crashing fury of the storm. It might, at any other
time, have seemed exaggerated, but not now. Quentin's
hands became searching as his mouth crushed hers,
touching every trembling part of her, then beginning
again, until helplessly responding, like someone drunk on
passion, Gina began exploring with her own hands the
hard, powerful muscles of his chest and back.

Murmuring his name under the pressure of his mouth,
she put her hands to his face, feeling the dominant male
contours of it. For her it was like a voyage of discovery
over a foreign land. Until now she had never touched a
man's face. That Quentin, whom she had known since
she was a child, could make her feel like this seemed a
miracle. Beneath his mounting passion she felt herself
coming completely alive. Never again would she be able
to look at him with a veil of innocence over her eyes. Her
skin was burning and a wild fever swept through her
blood. It was incredible the things she was becoming
aware of, simply because Quentin was kissing her.

Slowly he raised his head. He might have been as
stunned as she was by the feeling which raced between
them, because he didn't move. He stared down at her, his
eyes glazed, half hidden by thick lashes, as if for the first
time in his life he scarcely knew what he was doing.

'God!' he muttered thickly, his breathing quickening,
as though he had been running, 'I want you, Gina.
There's something about you——' Hoarsely his voice
trailed off, his mouth closing over hers again, forcing her
lips ruthlessly apart. His hands slid down to the curve of
her hips, thrusting himself against her as he felt her helpless surrender. Then he was bending over her, his hands
determined on her slender limbs.

Somehow, Gina didn't feel alarmed. She trusted him,
so she didn't even struggle. All she wanted was to please
him. He was so dear to her—hadn't she always loved

him? Who was she to refuse anything he asked? Never could she remember feeling so vulnerable yet so strangely acquiescent and excited.

Unconsciously careless of passion already moving towards the point of no return, she tightened her slender arms around his neck. A little murmuring sound escaped her, an instinctively feminine effort to placate his raging masculinity. Lovingly, with a natural seductiveness she wasn't aware of, she curved herself closer, giving herself up to the sureness of his expertise, his increasing demands.

It took a terrific crash of thunder, after which the heavens appeared to open, to bring Quentin to his senses, that and Gina's first whimper of pain. Gasping, he lifted his head. 'What the hell . . .?' he exclaimed, in livid self-disgust, pushing her harshly away from him.

As he did so, she was conscious of his thundering heart, the heat of his skin which might outrival her own, and was vaguely aware he was disturbed as well as angry. But while he had experience, she had nothing to guide her— nothing but instinct, which immediately let her down.

While she wanted to cling to him, the gap between them was suddenly unbridgeable. As he rose swiftly to his feet he was a stranger again, a man she might never have known. Her own emotions she ignored, being unable to accept she had just emerged from a child into a woman. If not in the fullest sense of the word, at least with a clearer understanding of what it was all about. In the darkness, in the arms of a man to whom she feared she mattered little, it seemed the last remnants of her childhood had disappeared for ever.

'Let's get back, Gina.' Quentin's face was a set mask.

He frightened her. 'Quentin?' she began haltingly.

'Be quiet!' His command might have been more acceptable if his voice hadn't been so curt. 'There's no real harm done, but we won't go into that. Just forget it.' The rain poured down as he slipped his sweater over her head, this time without deviation. It reached Gina's knees, providing adequate if slightly ludicrous protection.

'What will you do?' she whispered hoarsely, when she could breathe again.

'I'll manage,' he replied, keeping his eyes grimly averted from her small figure. 'Perhaps you can remember where it was you left your clothes? If you can't—well, it must be early morning. I doubt if there'll be anyone around when we get home.'

He sounded sarcastic about her clothes, as if he was deliberately trying to hurt her. His voice was hard edged, faintly explosive, and she swallowed weakly. 'I'm trying to remember . . .'

'You usually have a good memory.'

Now his voice contained a smooth insolence, his eyes a cruel glitter, but at least it helped her to pull herself together. For a moment she stood quite still, getting her bearings, then, after steadying her still trembling limbs, she was able to find, without much difficulty, the place where she had got undressed.

Obligingly, Quentin turned his back, though it was too dark to see and seemed slightly absurd after what had just taken place, while she scrambled into her jeans and shirt. Somehow she found his taut silence more hurtful and unnerving than the night.

As she returned his sweater with a brief murmur of thanks, both the wind and the rain increased in fury. 'Let's get out of here,' he urged again, adding with loaded cynicism, 'before anything else comes to stop us!'

The next morning being Sunday, Quentin didn't go to London. Often he spent his weekends away from home, either on business or pleasure, but there was some evidence that this weekend he intended to remain at Briarly. He was down at the stables early, and for once Gina found herself wishing he had had engagements elsewhere. It wasn't so much the kisses they had exchanged, although they had been enough to prevent her from sleeping, it was the fear that he might be about to turn her and her father out of their cottage that made her less than pleased to see him.

He came to stand beside her as she stood looking at Hector, his arm just touching hers along the top of the door, but otherwise detached. 'Any signs of improvement this morning?' he asked curtly.

'Yes, I think so.' Why, when Quentin's voice was so steady, did hers have to tremble like a leaf? Taking a firmer grip of herself, she added, 'Richard's a good vet—I'll say that for him.'

'Sometimes, Gina, you say far too much!' Quentin's sharpness startled her, almost as much as the hard glance he flung at her pale young face. 'It's not only what you say,' he continued, she thought unfairly, 'it's the things you get up to. The whole situation is becoming quite ridiculous.'

'I suppose you're referring to last night?' It took a lot of courage to look at him, but she managed it. Quentin, this morning, might look slightly haggard, but he still exuded a disturbing vitality which nothing appeared able to dim. Her heart reacted violently, beating over-rapidly as her anxious eyes fixed on his rigid mouth. Completely confused for a moment, she blurted out before he could answer, 'I'm sorry I made such a nuisance of myself in the storm, but if I seemed stupid it was because I'd never been kissed before. It was different from how I thought it would be.'

A glint of derision narrowed his eyes. 'You see what I mean when I say you talk too much?' he drawled tersely. 'You didn't have to bring that up again. Such incidents, my child, are better forgotten. And, while I refuse to believe it was your first kiss, how was it different?'

His tone had changed, becoming wary yet curious. Frowning slightly, she stared at him, colour staining her pale cheeks, her eyes mutely appealing. 'I'm not sure.'

'You aren't suggesting we try again?' The sneer in his voice told her just how much co-operation she could expect from him. 'It's not on, Gina. You don't have what I want, and never will,' his gaze swept contemptuously over her thin body. 'I would advise you not to start experimenting with other men, either. You might easily get more than you bargained for.'

She continued to stare at him, far too used to Quentin's arrogance to question it now. Painfully, at last, she asked, 'What if I'd fallen in love?'

'You're too young to be talking of love, Gina, and you certainly don't love me.'

Bleakly she retorted, 'I know you don't love me!'

He seemed gratified that she realised there wasn't the slightest possibility. His glance was harshly unkind. 'Would you expect me to, Gina? Even if you were properly dressed, you'd still be plain, and when I spare the time to take a girl out I like her to be decorative.'

It was rumoured that he was popular with women, that they spoiled him by running after him, leaving him to pick and choose. This must be true, and was perhaps why he spoke of them so carelessly. Gina gazed at him helplessly, in spite of his cruelly castigating words, loving him fervently.

When she didn't reply, he went on grimly, 'I imagine you thought the offer of a little love, last night, might prevent me from throwing you out of the cottage?'

'No, I didn't.' Surprise dilated her eyes to a lovely translucent green. 'I have more sense than to think that!' she assured him sharply.

He frowned. 'Miss Edgar's coming about eleven. We'll take the horses out then, so you'd better get the tack ready. But, first, I'm coming with you to see your father.'

'Why must you go near the cottage, Quentin?' she asked him bitterly.

'I've already told you.'

Suddenly she rounded on him fiercely, driven to desperation. 'Your father let us stay there because—because he said he owed John something. I think your father might have done something criminal and my father knew what it was. John is ill. If you go and disturb him you never know what he might do. Your father was greatly respected, Quentin. Surely you wouldn't want to risk ruining his good name, now that he's gone?'

Quentin's face darkened thunderously as he gripped her arm. 'Something tells me you aren't telling me the whole truth, Gina. You maybe don't know it, or maybe you're just trying to look after your own interests. Whatever it is I intend finding out.'

Miserably Gina trailed after him on the way to the cottage, praying she hadn't made things worse. If she had failed, she could only hope that John might do better, that he might be able to persuade Quentin to let them stay. If not—her mind boggled, refusing to go beyond this point.

John was up when they arrived and she saw at once that he was worse than usual. He looked grey and shrunken as he sat in a chair by the empty grate, and to her dismay his voice was slurred.

'Ah!' he glanced up as they walked in. 'Mr Hurst, I presume.' Neither man made any attempt to shake hands.

'We haven't met for a long time.' Quentin appeared to be making an effort to speak cordially. 'I didn't realise the cottage was in such a bad state. I'm afraid you'll have to move.'

For the first time in a long time, Gina recognised some expression in her father's eyes. He seemed oddly shocked, yet he managed to say smoothly, 'I'm sure you'll allow us to stay. Your father would have wished it.'

'I've been led to believe you knew something criminal about my father?' Quentin countered, giving Gina a hard look.

'Oh, no,' John Foster smiled thinly, while Gina prayed in vain. 'If you've been told that then your informant is wrong. Andrew believed I once saved his life, but it was nothing another man couldn't have done. It happened to be my job, I was there, and there was nothing remotely criminal about it.'

'And you're quite prepared to consider the debt no longer exists?' Quentin didn't, to Gina's relief, press to know details, and John didn't elaborate.

Listlessly he nodded. 'I never considered it existed. All the same, I don't want to leave this cottage.'

'I'm afraid you'll have to,' Quentin repeated, even more adamantly. 'Although I won't put you out until I've at least tried to find you alternative accommodation, and I'd appreciate it if you'd make some effort towards finding something yourself.'

John sighed querulously, turning cold, bloodshot eyes on Gina. 'Doesn't my daughter work hard enough for you? If you've any complaints I'll have a word with her, if you like.'

The silence in the ugly little room was brittle. Gina sensed Quentin's sudden fury, although she was puzzled to know what caused it. Perhaps, like her father, he had doubts regarding her work?

'I'll try to do better,' she promised eagerly, touching his arm.

Impatiently Quentin brushed her arm away. 'That has nothing to do with it,' he snapped grimly. Preparing to leave, he turned at the door. 'I'll be in touch, Foster. You can count on that.'

John Foster didn't reply. To Gina his face was grey and pathetic, and she hated Quentin's harsh inflexibility. John was down—anyone with eyes could see, and Quentin was taking a cynical delight in seeing him bereft of defences. Well, John still had some—he had her, she would never let him down!

'Don't worry,' she went to him, awkwardly patting his shaking hand, for he disliked being touched, 'I'll think of something.'

When she and Quentin returned again to the stables, he said he was going to get some breakfast. Since leaving the cottage Gina hadn't spoken. There seemed nothing left to say and she wasn't going to plead with him in the mood he was in, but apparently he believed she was sulking.

'I won't change my mind, Gina,' he informed her bitingly, 'so you'd better get used to the idea of moving on.'

'Yes,' she replied obediently, trying to still the hunger pangs she felt when he spoke of breakfast.

'What the hell's the matter with you?' he exclaimed in disgust, taking away her last bit of dignity. 'Your stomach's rumbling worse than Hector's. Haven't you eaten yet?'

'I'm—I'm going to,' she muttered, looking away from him.

In the momentary silence that followed, he observed her narrowly. 'You'd better come with me,' he said abruptly. 'It might be quicker for you than going all the way back home.'

Hastily she refused, thinking nervously of Mrs Worth, Quentin's cook-housekeeper, who ruled supreme in her kitchen. And Matthews, who would never tolerate her in his beautiful dining-room . . .

Her refusal, however, was just as quickly dismissed. Grasping her thin arm impatiently, Quentin dragged her along with him. 'Do you always have to argue?' he demanded curtly. 'You'll do as I say.'

He entered the back way, pausing in the kitchen, while Mrs Worth ran a disdainful glance over Gina's shabby clothes and the two maids raised dainty, fastidious eyebrows.

'Can you find Gina something to eat, Mrs Worth?' he

asked easily. 'The corner of the kitchen table will do. You don't have to put yourself out.'

Thus saying he left her, leaving Gina incredulous that her imagination had carried her as far as his dining or breakfast room. What a little fool she had been!

Cook and the two maids, whom she knew vaguely as Jean and Myra, were still staring at her as if she were something the cat had brought in. Matthews entered majestically, staring too, making it four against one. No one made any move to offer Gina anything to eat.

'I'm sorry,' she felt her face burning with humiliation, 'Quentin misunderstood me. I've already had my breakfast.'

She couldn't escape quickly enough, but no attempt was made to stop her. In fact, she fancied she heard their sighs of relief. Swiftly she ran back to the stables, tears streaming down her face, unable to prevent them. She buried her wet face against the neck of the little mare she was fond of. 'I could never have stayed there, Leonie, they all hate me.'

'Who does?' a light voice asked gruffly.

Startled, she turned. It was Richard. 'Oh, Richard!' her defences down for once, she collapsed against him, as he gently drew her away from the horse. 'I'm sorry,' she tried to smile as she made an effort to pull herself together, 'I was just feeling sorry for myself.'

He didn't let her go. His kindly face was anxious and his arm tightened protectively. 'You're too thin, Gina. Don't you ever eat anything?'

What was there about her this morning, she wondered, that both he and Quentin should suspect she was starving? 'Of course I eat.'

'Not going in for this silly slimming business, are you?'

Thinking of the empty shelves in the cottage larder, she gave a hollow laugh, shaking her head. 'Of course not.'

'I tell you what,' Richard's face lightened, 'come and

have breakfast with me at the Old Castle,' he named a luxury hotel a few miles away. 'I could do with something myself and I hate eating alone.'

It was a balm to her bruised spirits that there was someone who wasn't ashamed to be seen with her, and she was really sorry she couldn't accept. 'Miss Edgar is coming, you see, and Quentin likes everything especially nice for her.'

'Damn Quentin,' he said, or something that sounded very like it, but there was a shadow on Gina's expressive face which prevented him from arguing. 'Look here,' he brushed her hair back so he could see her better, 'I have a flask in the car, which I seldom have time for. Why not share it with me?'

Gina wanted to refuse again, but she hadn't the will-power and she was hungry. 'All right,' this time her smile wasn't forced. 'Thank you, Richard, I'd like that.'

'Then sit yourself down on those bales while I fetch it,' Richard grinned back.

CHAPTER THREE

FEELING better already, Gina waited, sitting like a small cat on the burnished bales of golden straw, letting the warm yellow sunshine, which stole in through the open window, wash over her. Richard brought a flask of coffee and a large packet of sandwiches, which his doting mother had packed for his lunch. She didn't notice he ate practically nothing while she scoffed almost the lot.

She ate greedily, revelling in the unexpected luxury of chicken and ham, and was nearly finished when Quentin strode in. To her astonishment his eyes went black when he saw her sitting with Richard, in the middle of what appeared to be a cosy feast.

'Making a pig of yourself, this morning, Gina?' he snapped, ignoring Richard. 'You have breakfast in my kitchen and another here. Didn't Mrs Worth give you enough?'

'I—I didn't have anything in your kitchen,' she stammered, not having been going to tell him.

'Why not?'

'I—I didn't feel I was welcome.' She hadn't meant to tell him that, either, for she feared Mrs Worth's reprisals.

'Wouldn't it be nearer the truth to say you saw Richard coming and couldn't wait to see him?'

Richard jumped to his feet, as angry now as Quentin. 'I'd like to think you were right,' he addressed Quentin curtly, 'but that's beside the point. I won't have you using that tone with Gina!'

'Won't you?' Quentin asked silkily.

'No, and I won't stand here and hear her insulted!'

Quentin's eyes were diamond-hard. 'Then we must do

something about it, mustn't we?' A hidden threat in his voice, he turned abruptly and left them.

They both stood staring as he disappeared, Gina frankly bewildered, Richard slightly puzzled as his anger faded.

'Don't take too much notice of him.' Gina tried to be soothing, while her heart jerked roughly. 'I don't think he's in a very good mood this morning.'

'Neither am I—now!' Richard rejoined grimly, taking a last look at Hector before gathering up his empty flask and leaving.

Gina had the horses groomed and waiting by the time Quentin reappeared with the ravishing Miss Edgar. Hector, left on his own, was very conscious of what he was missing and Gina felt sorry for him. Quentin spoke to him gently, and Gina, recalling how he had been earlier, marvelled. He had been brutal with her and John and offended Richard, yet here he was, talking to Hector, as though no wrong word had ever crossed his lips all morning!

It must be because of Miss Edgar, she supposed unhappily, secretly envious of Blanche's elegance. What must it be like to own clothes like those Blanche Edgar wore?

Quentin might have been thinking the same thing, as he helped her with the last two horses after seeing Blanche safely mounted. 'Couldn't you have smartened yourself up a bit?' he demanded coldly.

Gina sighed, feeling suddenly fed up by what she considered his continual references to her less than immaculate appearance. Clothes were only clothes, after all. 'Don't worry,' she retorted, unusually tart, 'I'll keep well behind.'

'You'd better.'

Angrily, Gina stepped back too quickly, bumping right up against Quentin's horse. They were just about to leave the stables and Quentin's other big horse, a light bay with a blaze on his face was highly strung. He reared, jerking back, practically throwing Gina into Quentin's arms.

Quentin's language was not too refined as he pulled Gina clear of the flying hooves. 'How many more times do I have to save your life before I get rid of you?'

The horse calmed down, but Quentin's breathing didn't, and as Gina stared up at him his face began to waver before her dazed eyes. She could feel her heart, the beat of his quickening, his mouth coming nearer, his eyes no less dazed of a sudden than her own. Her mind spun dizzily and from his parting lips came a sound like a half groan. Then Blanche was calling, in her rather high-pitched voice, and with a smothered oath Gina was free. Free, but curiously disembodied, as Quentin lifted her, flinging her almost savagely into her saddle.

The ride that morning seemed, to Gina, interminable. Quentin went in front and all she saw was his broad back. He rode with Blanche and was flatteringly attentive. He even paused once, when Blanche leaned flirtatiously towards him, to kiss her, being sure, Gina was sure, that she was looking. Blanche was in her early thirties, younger than Quentin and beautiful. Beside her Gina felt gauche, and she knew Blanche dismissed her as colourless and uninteresting. If ever she spoke to Gina she used extremely condescending tones and seldom waited for Gina's reply.

Watching her with Quentin, Gina sighed. There was no denying they made a handsome couple and she had heard that Quentin was looking for a wife. Someone who could help him socially. Blanche Edgar would be ideal, Gina admitted bleakly, and she wondered what made him hesitate. It was quite obvious that Blanche would be more than willing to accept him!

They had been riding for about an hour when they met

a neighbour who invited them for sherry. Gina was left
outside the large old manor house to keep an eye on the
horses, although Felix Duke protested.

'Wouldn't Gina care to come in as well? She's more
than welcome.'

'Gina has a job to do,' Quentin said suavely.

'I'll bring you something out, then,' Felix smiled at her
warmly.

Quentin's eyes narrowed, but he raised no further
objections as he helped Blanche dismount and they followed Felix inside.

Felix did bring Gina a sherry, a few minutes later. He
was a very presentable young man who, like Quentin and
Richard, lived with his mother. His parents were
divorced and this property had come to him through his
grandfather, but he farmed it well. Somehow Gina had
bumped into him a lot lately, when she was out with the
horses.

'Thanks,' she whispered, smiling at him, feeling un-
consciously wicked, as she sensed that for some reason,
Quentin didn't approve. As Felix lingered, she warned,
'Hadn't you better go back to your company?'

'I expect they're quite content with each other,' Felix
grinned. 'Anyway, Mother's there.'

She and Felix talked horses and it was pleasant just
standing in the summer sunshine with the sherry going
slightly to her head. Quentin didn't stay long, no longer
than fifteen minutes, and when he came out he wasn't
looking particularly cheerful.

Afterwards they returned to the stables and Gina
didn't see Quentin again that day. She wasn't surprised
at this, but she was surprised when the stranger who arrived next morning informed her that he was the new vet,
and had come to see the sick horse.

'Is Richard Hedley ill?' she enquired. It might be Richard's day off, but she thought he would have told her.

The new man looked slightly uncomfortable. 'I've no

idea, but I shouldn't think so. I'm not with his practice, I'm afraid. Seemingly, Mr Hurst fancied a change. It's not unheard of,' he added, appearing mildly amused at her growing indignation.

The new vet was competent enough, Gina was willing to concede, but she felt furious, and when Quentin turned up, later that evening, she tackled him. 'Why did you get rid of Richard?'

'Gina,' he exclaimed, with deceptive mildness, 'it's surely none of your business who comes to doctor my horses. And they are my horses, don't forget! I won't be dictated to by a little nobody like you.'

She closed her eyes tightly for a moment before opening them wide. 'I never try to dictate to you, but Richard is my friend and I—I feel I have the right to know.'

'Have you? I doubt it,' Quentin snapped.

While she had known he could be ruthless, she had never been so fully conscious of it before. 'Was it because he—he gave me something to eat?'

'I offered you breakfast myself yesterday, didn't I?'

'That—that was different.'

'I wish you'd lose your adolescent habit of stuttering and stammering! It certainly was different. I offered you a perfectly respectable meal at my kitchen table.'

'While Richard offered to share his, to sit with me.'

'In the straw.' Quentin's laughter was far from pleasant and his eyes glittered harshly.

Gina was incensed. 'He—he offered to take me to the Old Castle. So get that!'

'You're impertinent!'

Suddenly, in the face of such icy disapproval, Gina's courage failed her and she backed away from the coldness of his eyes. How could she explain to Quentin that he was the only man who mattered, but he would never give her friendship, let alone love! Richard was her friend and she would miss him, for she had few friends, but this was something Quentin couldn't be expected to understand.

'I'm sorry,' she whispered, her eyes filling with difficult tears. 'I know you have every right to choose your own vet, and I'll be able to see Richard whenever I want to . . .'

Quentin viewed her tears grimly. 'He means a lot to you?'

Gina hesitated. 'He's always been kind to me and he's good with Hector, and I shouldn't like his partners to think he hasn't been doing his job properly, as they may do when they discover you aren't satisfied with him.'

'I didn't give a reason, either good or bad, so I don't think you have anything to fear. People have been known to change their vets before, you know. As for seeing him outside,' Quentin went on coldly, 'that's up to you. What you do when you leave here is your own business.'

Immediately diverted from the subject of Richard, Gina struggled with an ache in her throat. 'So you still want me to leave?'

'Both you and your father,' he confirmed darkly. 'I have to go abroad this week, but I've already set the wheels in motion.'

Whatever did he mean? Her small face whitened, looking oddly pathetic. 'Whereabouts abroad are you going?' she asked wistfully, having never been farther than the nearest town, where she had been to school.

'Sydney,' he said briefly, staring at her, as if he wished to see her more clearly in the dim confines of the stable.

How lovely, she thought, to have had the right clothes, the right background, so that she might have gone with him. If she had belonged to the same social class as himself, he might not have disliked her so much. He might even have wanted to kiss her again. Tightly she closed her eyes to shut out the memory of the grassy bank by the lake. She was sure she could never bear to go there again.

'Gina?' The familiar impatience was in his voice as he rasped. 'Why do you keep closing your eyes while I'm talking to you?'

She certainly couldn't keep them closed when he spoke to her like that! With a start she opened them wide. He sounded exactly like her old form teacher at school. Rather than answering Quentin directly, she mentioned this with a faint smile.

'So you're lumping me with Anne Westcott now, are you? In her age group, I presume?'

'Age group?'

'She can't be a day under fifty.'

'Oh, no, Quentin,' Gina's green eyes became emerald pools of surprise, 'I never think of you as being that old, and I'd no idea you knew Miss Westcott?'

'I had the—er—pleasure of sitting on a committee with her once.'

Gina grinned, and Quentin Hurst's strong features relaxed. Suddenly they were laughing together warmly, in harmony, and it didn't seem wholly because of Miss Westcott. Quentin's white teeth glinted and the lines around his eyes creased. Then just as suddenly they stopped laughing and stared at each other again. Gina's breath caught as Quentin took a step forward.

It was then that Miss Edgar walked in and took Quentin away. She didn't need to persuade him, he seemed glad to go. As if the laughter he had shared with Gina had been a complete mistake, he turned as he went out and snapped coldly, 'Don't forget what I told you. Be ready to leave any time.'

Gina was up early to watch him depart for Australia. She concealed herself behind some thick trees on the drive opposite the house, where he couldn't see her. As he came through the front door, tall and elegant in his dark suit, she saw him pause to speak to Matthews, who was following. Her eyes were fixed on him intensely as he lowered himself into his car and switched the ignition. With a brief salute to Matthews he was off, passing within a few yards of Gina, without realising she was there.

Gina spent the rest of the day as she usually did, with

the horses. They were to feed and exercise and groom, and she had a special diet to prepare for Hector, and even a hot bran mash took time. That evening, after leaving the stables spotless, she went home, and an hour later her father was taken seriously ill. An ambulance was called, on Mrs Hurst's orders, after Gina ran back to the big house for help, and he was taken immediately to hospital. Gina went with him and, because she was quite alone and so young, they allowed her to stay with him. Most of the time she had to spend in the waiting room, but John Foster never regained consciousness. She was grateful, though, that she was there when he died, and, after a Sister had led her away, one of the doctors, who had fought for John's life, spoke to her.

'I'm sorry, my dear, there was so little we could do.'

'I should have known he was ill,' she whispered, completely numb with shock. 'He didn't seem to be talking properly, but I—I thought it was because he was drinking too much.' She had felt forced to tell the doctor about John's drinking habits when he was admitted, but she suspected they had already guessed.

The doctor looked at her anxiously. 'You mustn't blame yourself, you know. Your father's health was so bad he was fortunate to have lived as long as he did.'

They were very kind, but after a while Gina pulled herself together and returned to Briarly. There seemed nothing else she could do. She had lost John, but as he had been more like a stranger than a father, apart from a sense of shock and loss she felt little actual grief. That she wasn't overwhelmed with grief because he was gone seemed to hurt, irrationally, more than anything else. It must be a tragedy that a father and daughter could share the same roof and yet be so far apart. John had appeared to live continually in the past, and, in doing so, had got no joy from the present and even less when contemplating the future.

It surprised her that there was so little trace of him about the cottage, but he had been a man with tidy habits and few possessions. There were only his books, dull medical tomes, they seemed to Gina, which he had kept hidden in an old chest, as though frightened anyone would see them. Gina had wondered about these books until she had discovered her father's profession. Even now she found it difficult to believe he had been a surgeon—so difficult, that although her father was gone, she didn't mention it to anyone.

The funeral took place later in the week and she was the only mourner. Surprisingly, Mrs Worth came with her. Gina, fearing Mrs Hurst had ordered her to, said awkwardly that it wasn't necessary, but Mrs Worth insisted. Gina was humbly glad of her company. It rained all the time and she felt terrible, and was conscious of being near to fainting before it was all over.

At the cottage, to which no one tried to prevent her returning, she made herself some tea. She had found some money when, remembering Quentin's orders, she had begun clearing out John's room. There were only a few pounds, but enough to buy some food. It seemed ironic that now she could afford some food she didn't seem able to eat anything. Pushing her plate to one side, she stumbled to her feet, after putting a few lumps of sugar in her pocket for the horses.

A week after the funeral Mrs Hurst called her in. Gina had never had much to do with Quentin's mother. It might be true to say she scarcely knew her but, on the rare occasions when their paths had crossed, Mrs Hurst had always smiled. To Gina she was a vague but kindly figure, not at all like her arrogant son!

Now she faced her in the drawing-room, where she felt decidedly out of place. Nor was she sure that Quentin would have approved. Matthews certainly didn't. He stared down his long nose at her when she arrived,

straight from the stables, looking untidier than usual with
her face smudged and her hair all over the place, in spite
of her hurried efforts to tidy it up.

'Do come in, dear, and sit down.' Mrs Hurst didn't
notice Gina's appearance—she was more concerned with
what she had to say.

After waiting for Gina to sit down, and after asking
how she was getting on, she hesitated. 'I believe you
know my son is abroad?' When Gina nodded and came
out with a rather indistinct yes, she continued, 'He rang
from Australia two days ago, and asked how you were
managing with the horses, and naturally I mentioned
your father's death. I'm afraid,' again Mrs Hurst hesitated, this time even more anxiously, 'I'm afraid my son
left strict instructions that you aren't to go on living at the
cottage by yourself. Nor does he wish you to do any more
work at the stables.'

Gina's first reaction was to clench her small hands into
fists and stare down at the thick green carpet. The room
was elegant, luxuriously furnished, and she wondered if
Mrs Hurst had any idea what a struggle life could be.
Glancing at her now, at the beautifully coiffured head
and expensive dress, Gina thought not.

Then immediately she was ashamed of such thoughts.
The Hursts had worked for everything they had, and
even if they hadn't it was wrong of her to be envious. Mrs
Hurst, along with her elegance, was kind, which was
more, Gina decided bitterly, than could be said of Quentin!

Weakly shaken, she burst out illogically, 'I couldn't
leave straight away. Quentin must know I need time to
find something else to do. He doesn't seem to understand!'

Mrs Hurst frowned. 'I believe he said something about
another groom coming this week. Apparently it was
arranged before he left.'

So that was what he meant when he had talked of setting the wheels in motion? 'But what about me?' Gina cried, her face white. If she had had time to think about it, some kind of warning, her pride would have forbidden her to appeal to Mrs Hurst like this, but her strangled cry had escaped before she could prevent it. 'I'm sorry,' she whispered huskily, 'I shouldn't be worrying you about it.'

Mrs Hurst frowned a trifle uneasily at Gina's distressed young face. 'I don't really mind, dear. As a matter of fact, I've been giving you and your problems some thought. Otherwise I might have told you what Quentin said sooner.'

As Gina fidgeted nervously, Mrs Hurst cleared her throat delicately. 'I'm afraid I don't know you as well as perhaps I ought to, especially as you've lived here such a long time. My husband did tell me, of course, that he had met your father years ago, but unfortunately I've never been strong enough to interest myself greatly in too many things. I've always had to conserve my energy, you see. You do seem a bright young girl, though, and I wondered if you would care to come and work for me.'

'For you?' Gina's mind, full of anguish at the thought of having to leave Briarly, and her beloved horses, was shocked afresh—if in a different way. 'How could I come and work for you?' she stammered. 'Quentin wouldn't allow it. He wants me to go.'

'He would be thinking of you in connection with the stables.' Mrs Hurst's voice was suddenly brisker. 'I don't suppose he's thought of anything else. For myself, I could do with someone, a sort of personal maid, if you like. A girl who would be prepared to help me with my wardrobe and dressing, and things like that. Someone I could ring for during the night when I'm not feeling well, or through the day to run errands for me. Fetch and carry, that sort of thing. All the things I could have asked a daughter to do, but unfortunately I never had one. I only have a son, and Quentin,' she finished, with a loud, rather self-pitying sigh, 'never has much time for me.'

'Mother!'

It would have been difficult to have discovered who was the most startled, Mrs Hurst or Gina, as they swung round simultaneously to find Quentin standing in the doorway behind them. Neither of them had heard the door open, and Gina thought that to say he looked furious would have been putting it mildly! His face was hard and there were deep lines of disapproval around his sensuous mouth. Gina was struck dumb with an immediate sense of shock, but while his eyes glittered over her darkly, she found it impossible to look away.

He looked strained, as if he had travelled a long way and gone a long time without sleep. His dark hair was ruffled and it seemed he must have discarded his jacket and driven from London without it. And while this might have been cooler for him, she could see patches of sweat over his broad shoulders, as if he had driven both himself and his car hard.

Mrs Hurst, after Quentin's defamatory exclamation, was the first to break the tense silence—which she clearly failed to understand. 'Why, Quentin!' she exclaimed, with a belated smile, 'this is a surprise! Do come in, you're causing a draught. I didn't expect to see you back so soon, but you don't have to look so angry, surely? I was just talking to Gina.'

'So I heard!' Coldly he interrupted his mother's hasty flow of words, his own weighted.

Gina, glancing uneasily from one to the other, remained silent.

'You've had a good journey?' Mrs Hurst ventured uncertainly. 'You must have managed quite a lot in a very short time?'

'Yes.' Quentin's reply was extremely non-committal. Gina felt rather sorry for his mother.

'Well then,' Mrs Hurst went on brightly, 'perhaps Gina and I should go to the library and continue the little discussion we were having there? Unless you're going straight upstairs?'

He nodded briefly. 'After you've explained what you were talking about when I came in.'

Mrs Hurst stopped smiling and drew a slightly peevish breath. Clearly she wasn't pleased at being dictated to in front of Gina. 'If you insist,' she murmured stiffly.

'I do.'

'Oh, very well!' She paused petulantly for a frowning moment then began. 'Gina and I feel we could help each other. I've asked her to come and work for me as my personal maid. Of course I realise she will have to be trained, but I'm sure she'll soon learn. She's young and intelligent and her voice is nice. It certainly doesn't grate, like that of some I could mention!' She gave a quick glance past Quentin through the door as if suspecting the constantly chattering Myra might be listening.

'My God!' Quentin stepped inside the room, quickly closing the door behind him. Obviously he had something to say and was going to make sure no one overheard. Gina suspected the direction of his mother's glance had warned him someone might, if he stayed where he was. As he came nearer she shrank back, as the full force of his anger became apparent. 'Mother,' he exclaimed, with deceptive softness, 'I don't know what crazy idea you have in mind, but Gina is certainly not coming to work here!'

'Why—why ever not?' Mrs Hurst seemed astounded.

'Because I say so!'

'But why not?' Mrs Hurst persisted. 'She could at least stay until she finds something else.'

'She's going to find something else, very quickly,' he assured his mother grimly, his eyes dwelling on Gina so coldly she shivered. 'I'll see to it myself.'

'But not here?' This time it was Gina who spoke, with the odd feeling that she must try to defend herself. Yet before his contempt she felt utterly miserable, her voice only defiant because she thought she had nothing to lose.

'I'll tell you why you can't stay here!' Reprovingly, Quentin lashed out at her, as if glad of the chance to attack her directly. 'I don't think you would know how to conduct yourself in a house. You've grown too used to living in a hovel, even though I'm ashamed to admit it belongs to me. As for being my mother's personal maid— if she really feels in need of such a thing—I doubt if you would know how to go about this either. You don't even know how to look after yourself! From what I've seen of you, you rarely even look clean.'

'But I am! I am clean,' Gina cried, mortally wounded, as his cold insults descended on her innocent head. With anguished eyes she gazed at him. 'You know I am!' She hadn't meant to remind him of the lake and hoped, suddenly uneasy, that he wouldn't connect it. His brain, however, was razor-sharp and, as she watched despairingly, a dull flush crept over the hard line of his jaw.

His glance flickered, before returning to ice. 'I still maintain you are ill fitted for the kind of work my mother has in mind.' With studied insolence, his brows rose cynically. 'Why don't you go and take a look at yourself? Your hair's a mess, your face is as grubby as usual. As for your hands, the less said about them the better! And don't say I haven't mentioned it before—and for all the notice you've taken I might as well have saved my breath.'

As if to ward off such an onslaught, Gina clasped taut arms across her breast. Her eyes went bright, the green turning to emerald, as she blinked back the tears which threatened to fall. 'It's often difficult to keep clean in the stables,' she whispered. 'I've tried to do better since——' she faltered, then made herself go on, determined that Quentin shouldn't think she was trying to make him feel sorry for her, 'since my father, died, but there still seems such a lot to do.'

For a moment Quentin's face paled grimly and his eyes shadowed, with what she thought was concern, but she realised she was mistaken when his voice came as curt as ever.

'I'm sorry about your father, Gina, but it alters nothing. I know what would happen if I let you stay here. You'd be running around the house making a perfect nuisance of yourself, quite incapable of helping anyone. You may think I'm hard, but you'll be grateful in the long run.'

Hastily, Mrs Hurst intervened, having given up trying to decide what was making Quentin so disgruntled. She was well aware he could be very decisive and high-handed when something didn't suit him, but usually he was fairly tolerant with his employees at Briarly. His London office was another thing, but that didn't concern her. She was concerned now, as she saw her wonderful dream of owning a willing little slave fast disappearing.

'Darling,' she murmured wistfully, 'I do think you're being too hard on the child. You've just said, yourself, she's never had a chance, living in that dreadful cottage with a father who just didn't care. Once she was working for me, after a few weeks, anyway, if her father was able to come back he probably wouldn't be able to recognise her.'

Her eyes seeming stretched to capacity, Gina stared at Mrs Hurst, feeling suffocated by a peculiar sensation. On one hand she was hit by Mrs Hurst's rather careless if well-meant references to her father, and on the other by Quentin's mounting animosity. She felt she had to escape. Turning too quickly, she made to rush past him when, suddenly, the room began swinging around her, whirling upside down and she with it. There was the same awful sensation which she had felt when she had been drowning in the lake, just before Quentin had rescued her. Now a similar feeling enveloped her overwhelmingly, and, as she fell into inky darkness, terrified, she called his name.

When she came to she was in bed, with Myra, the
dark-haired, voluble little housemaid, bending over her.

'I thought you were waking up!' she exclaimed.

'Why—why am I here?' Gina was dazed, only able to
realise she was in a strange bedroom. She waited until her
eyes cleared, to make sure she wasn't dreaming, but
Myra's face stayed, so did the bedroom. Confused, she
gazed around. The room was beautiful, but she didn't
recognise anything. 'I shouldn't be here,' she whispered
anxiously.

'Stop worrying!' Myra advised, but stared at her curiously. 'Mr Quentin carried you here himself, so if I were
you I wouldn't argue. Said something about you coming
to work for his mother and having to be near her, but I
hope I never see him looking like that again. Like
murder, he looked, I can tell you, and sent us all away.
Wouldn't let one of us touch you!'

'For fear you got the plague,' Gina muttered bitterly.

'What's that?' Myra's brown eyes sharpened.

'Oh, nothing.' Wondering why she felt so weak, Gina
struggled to sit up. Then, seeing she had nothing on, she
immediately pulled the sheet up over her bare shoulders,
in an attempt to cover herself. 'What time is it?' she
asked, colouring helplessly.

'Nine o'clock in the morning,' Myra informed her
coolly. 'You've slept a long time, but Mr Quentin
wouldn't let us wake you.'

'Nine o'clock in the morning!' Gina felt a shock of dis-
belief go right through her. 'It can't be?'

'There's the clock!' Myra waved a hand at it indifferently. 'You don't have to believe me.'

Gina did. There was no reason for Myra to lie to her.
'Where are my clothes?' she asked blankly. 'I'd better get
up.'

'On the floor,' Myra answered obligingly. 'You must
have left them there last night and I haven't picked them
up. That's one of the first things you'll have to learn if

you're coming to work here, to be tidy. None of us are going to run after you—and it will pay you to remember.'

'I don't want you running after me,' Gina tried to assert with dignity. 'All I want is to be left alone for a few minutes, while I get dressed.'

'The bathroom's next door, but I've had orders to stay with you until you get dressed, then take you downstairs,' Myra shrugged. 'You're such a skinny little thing, Cook says she'll have to fatten you up if you're to work for Mrs Hurst.'

Gina had thought there must have been some mistake when Myra had talked of her working for Quentin's mother. Now she knew it must be true. Flinging back the bedclothes, no longer caring much that she was naked, she cried fiercely, 'I shan't be working for Mrs Hurst, or anyone else around here. I'm going straight downstairs to see Quentin!'

'You are?' Myra began to perk up. 'Then I'll leave you to it, or he'll be accusing me of egging you on. And I don't want the blame for anything, not if he's in the same mood as he was in last night.'

'Don't worry, it hasn't anything to do with you,' Gina made an effort to control her impulsive temper. 'I just want to tell him I'm going.'

'Okay, okay!' Myra was already halfway through the door. 'I've done my bit.' Spitefully she paused. 'Better you than me. And, if you've any appetite left after His Nibs is finished with you, breakfast's ready in the kitchen.'

Gina's short burst of anger gave her the strength to throw on her clothes, after Myra had gone, and rush downstairs. She did spare another puzzled glance for the gracious comfort of the bedroom, but, otherwise, she didn't even pause to do more than run a careless comb through her heavy mop of red hair. It wasn't until she was halfway downstairs that she stopped to think. It was only then, when she gave it a chance, that everything

came rushing back and she slid to an apprehensive halt,
incredulous that she could have forgotten. Then, with a
despairing gasp, she sat down where she stood, slumped
against the beautifully carved stair rail, while her spirits
sank with her small bare feet into the thick carpet beneath her.

CHAPTER FOUR

WHEN Gina woke up her mind had been a blank, with reality clouded, but now the events of the night were beginning to return so clearly that she recoiled, wishing she were back in her dream world again.

It seemed impossible that she could have forgotten the conversation she had had with Quentin, after she had come round to find him sitting by her bed. On opening her eyes, she had wondered hazily where she was and why he was there. When she had remembered properly she had concluded that he must be waiting to make sure she was still in one piece, after the way he had attacked her. Whether he had been worried about her or not, he hadn't said, but the hate in her green eyes must have assured him he hadn't done any fatal damage.

He had made her drink something peculiarly obnoxious. She had suspected it was poison, although if it had been it couldn't have worked, because she was still alive this morning. The mixture he had given her must have been responsible for her brief lapse of memory, though. Otherwise, wouldn't she have recalled the awful things he had thrown at her before now?

There had been no one else around—the house quiet and sleeping, only the clock, far down in the hall, chiming out the hour of one. Gina had no idea if it had been Quentin who had put her to bed. She had felt warm and comfortable, disinclined to ask questions and curiously resentful that he should be sitting beside her, reminding her painfully that, for all he might appear concerned, she had no real place in his life.

Then, suddenly, as he put down the glass he had held

for her, they had been quarrelling fiercely, about almost everything. Furiously she had tackled him about the stables, the horses, the cottage and her right to stay there, if she pleased. Free of his mother's restrictive presence, Gina had argued until her breath came in gasps and her eyes filled with angry tears, but to no avail.

Like a man made of steel, Quentin had worn her down, battering her with indisputable facts until she had realised she was beaten. She might have known this from the start, but she had been bolstered by the incredibly foolish hope that she might bluff him into submission. The boot, unfortunately, had been on the other foot. Bitterly, Gina reflected how she was the one who had been forced to give in—in a welter of humiliation. Quentin had held all the cards, she just didn't have a chance. In the end, fearing she had said too much and, by doing so, had merely strengthened his resolve to send her away, she had buried her pride and humbly begged to be allowed to stay, promising meekly to do anything he asked.

He had stared at her angrily, then surprisingly agreed—if like someone questioning their own sanity. 'But only if you're prepared to stay out of my sight,' he warned curtly. 'And if you're so determined to become a servant, then you'd better begin conducting yourself like one. How are you going to like eating all your meals in the kitchen, and bowing to Matthews instead of mentally pulling a face at him each time he gives you a disapproving glance? And having to call me Mr Quentin, as no doubt my mother will ask you to do?'

As he paused enigmatically, she stared at him uneasily, but it seemed he hadn't yet finished. 'I'm sorry your father died, Gina, in more ways than one. I didn't expect he would go so suddenly and I'm afraid it's upset my immediate plans for you. But as long as you keep out of my way you can stay here until you've had time to make plans of your own. However, don't come running to me for help when my mother's demands wear you out. She

doesn't want a maid, she wants a slave, and never tell me
I didn't warn you. And tidy yourself up. I won't have
anyone on the indoor staff looking as you do. Oh, and
another thing, keep away from the stables.'

This, to Gina, seemed a worse punishment than anything else. 'Please,' she whispered, her face strained, her
eyes huge with sudden tears, 'couldn't I just go occasionally, to see Hector?'

He had turned his head away, as if the sight of her had
offended him too much. 'No, you may not! And the new
man has his orders.' He turned back to her, his own face
taut. 'It will be no use your chasing after him as you did
with Richard. Jenkins will immediately report to me.'

'You've thought of everything, haven't you?' she had
retorted hotly, unwisely discovering her vanquished
pride. With tormented eyes she had looked at him, so tall
and autocratic, leaning over her. 'I think,' she'd whispered tearfully, 'I'm beginning to hate you. I thought I
was beginning to love you, but I'm glad now that I've
discovered my mistake.'

For an instant the line of his mouth went rigid, as he
took in her tearful desperation, the wealth of electrical
emotion between them that clearly confused her. 'Hate
might be wiser for you just now,' he replied harshly,
'until you learn to grow up a bit. I doubt if you know the
true meaning of love, or that you could cope with all its
implications.'

'I don't suppose you know much about it either?' Gina
retorted bitterly, a pulse hammering helplessly in her
throat. 'I can't imagine you ever being in love.'

'Oh, I don't know,' he frowned darkly, his breath
fanning her cheek like a threat before he drew sharply
back. Coolly, as he controlled himself, his glance went
over her thin arms and bosom, staying on the latter, as if
held in spite of himself. 'I might surprise you one of these
days.'

'Blanche?' she sighed deeply, feeling pain.

'Gina!' he said thickly, then paused abruptly, as though refusing to contemplate another argument. 'I'm going to leave you now,' he rose grimly to his feet, 'but don't forget what I've said. You can stay, but only if you learn to keep out of my way and tidy yourself up.'

He had gone, closing the door quietly behind him, but with that same touch of violence she had noticed on the night by the lake, when he had held her and crushed her, as though he had little control left.

Suddenly, as Matthews hovered in sight, Gina jumped to her feet, rushing back upstairs. She wasn't sure if Quentin was still in the house, but she could see no point in confronting him now, not when she had recalled their conversation in the bedroom. She, had two options, it seemed. She could either go or stay, and, as she had no-where to go, obviously she had no real choice!

The next few weeks passed slowly, and if in the past Gina had occasionally thought her lot a hard one, she considered it a lot more preferable to her life now. As Quentin had warned, his mother, though never actually unkind, made her fetch and carry for the greater part of each day. Through the night, too, the bell connecting Gina's room with hers, often rang, and Gina was forced to leave her bed and go and see what it was Mrs Hurst wanted. Usually it was nothing more than a hot drink and a little chat to while away a dark hour, but for Gina it meant lost sleep, at a time when perhaps she most needed it.

She had managed to tidy herself up, as Quentin had insisted, but gazing in her mirror she could see no great improvement. At least it was easier to keep clean now she didn't work in the stables, and her skin was so fine it didn't seem to matter that she had no make-up. It was her hair that was as thick and long as ever, so she simply tied it back and covered it with the old-fashioned mob-cap that Mrs Hurst insisted on her wearing.

Mrs Hurst hadn't said anything about wages, while she

was training, but she did get her board and her clothes. Her clothes consisted of several of Mrs Hurst's cast-off dresses, some unworn, which Mrs Worth obligingly altered to fit Gina's more petite figure. The result was far from flattering because Mrs Worth was no great needle-woman, but Gina decided they were better than nothing and, as Mrs Hurst pointed out, the material was good.

Mrs Hurst often sighed over her, with the air of one sore tried, but Gina forced herself to endure her disparaging comments silently. It was much the same in the kitchen, where Myra and Jean took a delight in tormenting her. They were apparently jealous of the smart bedroom she had been given and wouldn't listen when Gina insisted she was there just so she could be near Mrs Hurst during the night. They considered she should have been at the back of the house with the rest of the staff, and their spiteful remarks often made Gina miserable.

So did Miss Edgar's—when Miss Edgar came across her one day in the gardens. Mrs Hurst, who was suffering from one of her migraines, had gone to lie down, which meant that for a while Gina was free. Unable to resist the temptation, she had gone to sit by the lovely fountain in the rose garden. She was well aware she shouldn't be there, but as it was Saturday and the gardener wasn't around, she didn't think anyone else would notice. She rarely ever saw Quentin, and if she did it was usually at a distance.

This Saturday, however, just as Gina was beginning to relax by the fountain pool, she was startled to see him coming round the nearest corner with Blanche Edgar. Before Gina could retreat they were pausing beside her, Blanche with a frown.

'Whatever is your little stable girl doing here, darling?' she pretended to stare at Gina more closely. 'It is your stable girl, isn't it? I thought you had a man now?'

'Yes, I have,' Quentin's voice was cold, but no colder than his eyes, as they rested on Gina. 'Gina still works

here, though, as a kind of personal assistant to my
mother.'

'So that's how she comes to be taking her ease in your
garden?' Blanche's laughter came, lightly malicious. 'Do
you think your mother's being wise, Quentin? I do see
her point, but I shouldn't have advised her to employ an
untrained girl.'

'Don't worry,' he took her arm, drawing her away
abruptly, 'Gina knows her place.'

Gina felt she was certainly learning it, but she often
found it far from easy. Why had she imagined it would be
easy? Once she had thought nothing would be too difficult, if only she could stay at Briarly beside Quentin.
Now she wasn't so sure. As she sat by the fountain,
watching him slip an arm through Blanche's, as they
walked away from her across the lawns, she knew she
must leave. Unfortunately she didn't know where to
begin—how to go about it. Without money it might be
impossible to go anywhere. Yet how could she stay here
and endure the mysterious but terrible pain which attacked
her heart, each time she saw Quentin with Miss Edgar?

It was inevitable that such unhappiness should make
her restless, and one night, after settling Mrs Hurst in bed
with a book and a cup of hot tea, she decided to risk
Quentin's wrath and go down to the stables. He had gone
for a short walk after dinner. She knew of this, because
Mrs Hurst had told her. Now he was in his study and it
was unlikely that he would go out again.

Somehow Gina didn't care all that much if he did. It
was a risk she was prepared to take. She had a sudden
longing to see Hector and the other horses, to get away
from the house for even a short time. Once, when she had
gone to the stables in daylight, the new groom had looked
extremely uncomfortable and had refused to say more
than a few words to her. She didn't think he had mentioned her visit to Quentin, but rather than get him into
trouble, she hadn't gone again.

The moon shone so brightly, she wished she hadn't chosen a night when it was full. She still had a stable key, which she had kept hold of deliberately, and using it she quickly unlocked the door. Hector, recognising her immediately, whinnied loudly with excitement.

'Hello, boy,' she whispered, hushing him anxiously, 'Hi! Don't make such a noise, unless you want to wake everyone up.'

'I told you not to come here, Gina!' Quentin's voice cut through the shadows behind her, as she stood with her arms around Hector's neck.

She almost died from shock and her slight body tensed. Swiftly she turned to the dark height of him as he approached her. 'I—I thought you were in the study?' she faltered.

'Apparently I'm not,' he retorted sarcastically. 'If I'd known you intended sneaking down here, I might have been more obliging.' Grimly he held out his hand. 'I'll have that key, Gina, if you don't mind.'

Childishly she put it behind her back, clasping it tightly in her hands. 'I'm sorry, Quentin—I mean Mr Quentin,' she refused stubbornly, 'I—your father gave it to me, but I promise I won't use it often.' Her voice shook a little, at what she knew was illogical defiance, but she forced a harder note into it. 'I have to come here sometimes to see the horses, you know that!'

Ignoring the mute appeal in her eyes, he replied curtly, 'It would be better for you if you stayed away.'

She shrugged, keeping a tight hold of the key, hoping he would forget it. 'I can't see how, but I suppose, now that I've broken the rules, you'll want me to leave?'

'Leave?'

'Briarly.'

'Oh, I see,' he sighed. Gina heard it clearly and wondered why he sounded so restive. 'Well, you'll have to, one day soon. You can't stay here indefinitely.'

She knew that, yet she couldn't admit he was right.

Turning her head, she rested it against Hector, leaning on his strength. 'Your mother likes having me around. She would miss me.'

'Naturally,' he said dryly. 'She finds it extremely pleasant to have you running after her continually, but it can't go on.'

'Why can't it, Quentin?'

'For heaven's sake, grow up, Gina,' he glared at her, his eyes glinting. 'You know you're wasting your time, your life here, as well as being a perfect pest. As soon as I get something sorted out . . .'

'You said that two weeks ago,' she interrupted.

'So what? These things take time,' he snapped. 'And I've more important things to think about.'

'Blanche, I suppose?' Gina was aware she was being impertinent, but his coldness provoked her.

'Perhaps,' he said.

'I suppose you're going to marry her?'

'I could do worse,' he agreed.

Wounded by this, and the grimness of his voice, she hung her head, feeling the sharpness of pain all over. It was a beautiful midsummer's evening, the air soft and heady with the scent of roses from the distant gardens, but she felt too dejected to appreciate such things. All she could think of was Quentin and Blanche.

'Gina!' he spoke her name on a note of exasperation. 'You'd better go to bed, but first give me that key.'

'No!' She had used it for years—she could never give it to him. It was all she had left to remind her of all the years she had spent here. To part with it would be like parting with a piece of herself. 'No!' she exclaimed again, trying to dodge around him.

He caught hold of her, to try and take it from her by force, his face hard and angry, and she was aware of the lean, muscular body wrestling with hers. Then he seemed to forget all about the key, as his hands tightened on her waist, as she fell against him with a strangled cry of indignation.

'Give me what I want,' he whispered hoarsely.

'The key?' Her voice was muffled, and she could feel her heart hammering against her ribs, filling her ears with the same thunder she had heard by the lake.

'Yes, Gina!' He slid a hand through the tangled mass of her hair and she knew vaguely that the key wasn't important any more, though it was what they both talked about. His hand pressed against the nape of her neck and with a sigh she pressed closer against him. He lowered his head as she raised hers, their movements, like clockwork, fitting together. Their lips touched, gently at first, then clung hungrily.

The pressure of his mouth was hard and cool. She couldn't understand how it could light such fires within her. Against his chest, her small but perfect breasts grew taut, while, contrarily, every bone in her body melted. She seemed to be flowing into him, her senses reeling as his hands and mouth moved insistently over her, in a way she remembered, then were suddenly, dramatically still.

As his mouth left hers Quentin lifted his head and she heard the harshness, the rejection in the breath he drew, moments before he thrust her away.

She felt him shaking, yet he glared down at her with hate in his eyes. 'What's the matter?' she asked.

'Nothing's the matter,' he ground out savagely, 'but there soon might be if you don't get out of my sight.'

'Very well,' her voice trembled. 'Don't think I'll not be glad to. And I'll promise not to tell Miss Edgar.'

'Blanche?' he muttered. 'What in the hell has she to do with it?'

'That's not a question you should be asking me. I'm only the girl you can't wait to get rid of. She's the one who'll be here to stay, remember?'

'Gina . . .!' he groaned, but she didn't wait to hear

more. The key was still in her possession and while Quentin's mind was on other things she escaped. That he was momentarily distracted provided a chance which seemed too good to waste.

Back in her room, gazing at the key before hiding it tearfully away, she wondered how she had come to hate Quentin so easily. There was love, too, but this she refused to acknowledge, preferring to concentrate on her hate and thoughts of revenge. Quentin was in a position to hurt her badly, but some time in the future, if she were patient, she might somehow get a chance to hurt him.

Gina was surprised, a few days later, when Mrs Hurst unexpectedly sent for her. As it was Saturday Quentin was at home, and when he was his mother liked to have lunch with him, and have coffee afterwards with him in the library. She often said it was one of the few opportunities she got for discussing her domestic affairs with him.

Gina had just finished her own lunch, although she had found it difficult to eat much. Ever since her encounter with Quentin in the stables she had felt depressed, but when Mrs Worth asked if there was anything wrong she pretended it was only a headache.

'You're wanted in the library,' Matthews told her ponderously as he entered the kitchen.

'Was that Sir Charles Hearn you were showing in?' asked the irrepressible Myra.

'It's none of your business, young lady,' Matthews sniffed, 'but yes, it was.'

'Wonder what he's after?' Gina heard Mrs Worth murmur idly, as she left the room.

Between Matthews and herself there was a kind of unspoken truce, but he still frowned on her more than he smiled, and the frown was very much in evidence today as, in the course of duty, he came along to open the library door for her and to close it behind her quietly.

Once inside Gina paused, selfconsciously adjusting her

mob-cap. She recognised Sir Charles Hearn from having
seen him at the stables. It must have been about two
years ago. He had been interested in a horse they had
had for sale, but he hadn't bought it, and she couldn't
recall seeing him since. She did remember Quentin's
father saying that Sir Charles lived on the other side of
Dorking.

He was standing. He had rather surprised her by
jumping to his feet as she came in, and she suddenly realised he was staring at her closely. He appeared so
shocked that she began feeling uncomfortable and was
relieved when she heard Quentin suggesting quietly to Sir
Charles that he should sit down again.

Gina wondered why everyone was watching her so intently. No one had spoken to her, but they all seemed to
be gazing at her in a very peculiar fashion. Indeed, Sir
Charles looked incapable of speech, although his mouth
worked strangely, and she was curious to know what it
was about her that was affecting him so oddly. Why, she
wondered, had he called?

Tearing her eyes from Sir Charles's anguished ones, she
turned uncomfortably to Quentin's mother. 'Matthews
said you wanted to see me, Mrs Hurst.'

It was as though the sound of her voice broke the dam
of shock and amazement that was struggling for release
inside Sir Charles Hearn. As Quentin took a grim step
towards her, Sir Charles was there before him, stunning
her by swiftly removing her cotton cap with trembling
hands.

As Gina, in astonishment, tried to prevent him, he exclaimed with an alarming hoarseness, 'I knew it! As soon
as she came through the door, I knew she couldn't be
anyone else but my granddaughter. This hair would confirm it, if nothing else did!'

His hands, touching lightly and excitedly on Gina's
startled head, came to rest on her tense shoulders. She
could feel his hands shaking, as though he was unable to

stop them, and, suddenly nervous, she cast a bewildered glance at Quentin. She might hate him but, instinctively, he was the one she looked to for help.

Yet it was Quentin's face, as she waited apprehensively for him to refute Sir Charles's crazy statement about her being his granddaughter, that startled her most. His face was a frozen mask, so pale that she had an immediate premonition of disaster. What had she done now to deserve such a look? He was staring at her as if she was someone he had never seen before. Uneasily she tried to wriggle from under Sir Charles's detaining hands.

Then suddenly her attention was wrenched from Quentin by the astonishing words which began falling thickly from Charles Hearn's thin lips. 'Yes, you're Virginia's child, right enough. There can be no mistake. And to think I've been living so near to you all these years and had no idea!'

'You're sure, Charles?'

To Gina's ears, Mrs Hurst's voice sounded slightly incredulous. She felt a little like that herself.

'Yes, Lydia,' Charles nodded decisively. 'Even without seeing her the evidence is indisputable. No doubt about it. I'm in possession of the full facts and once I saw her I knew. It was like watching my own daughter—or no . . .' he hesitated, 'my mother, whom I believe Gina closely resembles, coming back to life. She has the same bones, the same hair, the same beautiful slightness. Oh, my dear child!' He bent his handsome old head gruffly to kiss her cheek, exclaiming again, 'To think you've been so near and I didn't know!'

Gina, drawing back apprehensively, could only feel relieved that he didn't try to hold her any closer. She found it almost impossible to believe that this distinguished, immaculately dressed man could be her grandfather. Staring at him nervously, she wasn't at all sure she wanted to believe it. Vaguely she was conscious that it might mean change, leaving Briarly and Quentin. And while it was one thing to decide she would leave, each time she quarrelled with him, it was quite another to have to actually do it. Again, her eyes full of desperate, silent appeal, she looked to him for help.

Charles Hearn's face was filled with intense excitement, but Quentin's was deathly pale. He was staring at Gina as if he understood her confusion but wasn't sure what to do about it. She heard his harshly drawn breath. 'I think it might be a good idea, Charles, if you began at the beginning and explained to Gina what this is all about. You can't expect her to be anything but bewildered until you do.'

'Of course, of course, what a fool I am!' Sir Charles cleared his throat. 'I should have thought of that, I'm going far too fast for her,' he exclaimed, as Quentin guided them stiffly to a nearby sofa.

Surely, Gina pondered silently petrified, if this had been true my father would have told me?

Quentin withdrew, announcing that he would get them all a drink, grimly ignoring the hand Gina held helplessly out to him, while Sir Charles never took his eyes off her face.

'You won't believe it,' he smiled, as Gina brought her reluctant attention back to him, 'that for years you've never been far from my thoughts, but now that I've found you I don't know where to start.' Then he sobered, and into her amazed ears poured what seemed to her a tragic and wholly regrettable story.

It appeared her real name was Sinton, not Foster. Her father had been Leo John Sinton, and he had married Gina's mother, Sir Charles's only child, when he was struggling in his first years after medical school.

'I didn't object to them marrying, but Virginia was so young, I begged them to wait. Unfortunately your father decided it was because I didn't think he was good enough for my daughter and he never forgave me.' Sir Charles sighed. 'He was a good surgeon, but because of our quarrel he became very bitter. He seemed determined that one day he would be wealthier than me, and drove himself beyond normal limits. Eventually, however, because of being overtired, he made a fatal mistake. A child died and he never forgave himself; he vowed he would never operate again.'

'That's why he came here?' Gina asked.

'It must have been, but he didn't come here until after your mother died. Things became so bad in London that she decided to go and stay for a few weeks with some friends in Mexico. You were only a baby and I fully expected she had taken you with her. When her plane crashed and she was killed I thought you had died too.' Charles paused, his face creased with remembered pain. 'I checked, but at the best of times in that huge country it's difficult to get accurate information. It was a shock, two years later, I can tell you, to meet your father carrying you down Oxford Street.'

'What did you do?' Gina was enthralled, in spite of herself, at last beginning to feel the story had something to do with herself.

'I immediately offered to take you, but he wouldn't hear of it, and I couldn't think of any way I might force him to hand you over, as grandparents have few legal rights, I'm afraid. I sensed, fortunately, that he was short of money and between us we reached some sort of agreement. It was crazy, in the middle of a London street, but I daren't let him out of my sight. I persuaded your father to accept a monthly allowance, ostensibly for you, and in return he promised to arrange that I should be told if ever anything happened to him. It seemed the best I could do,' Charles sighed, 'but every day since then has been an anxious one.

'Fortunately, though, he honoured his word. Unfortunately, however, the solicitor with whom he drew up this agreement was away when your father died, or I should have known sooner. You can guess the shock I

received when I realised you'd been living so near me all
the time. He always threatened, you see, that if I ever
tried to contact you he would make sure I never saw you
again. But it's difficult to believe he never mentioned me
to you, Gina, or said anything to you about your mother.'

'No,' quite stunned now by these revelations, Gina
shook her head, 'he told me nothing, but Mr Hurst,
Quentin's father, did tell me my father had been a well
known surgeon. I wondered why he had told me, at the
time. He seemed rather worried about it. Perhaps he
hoped to force John into telling me the truth?'

Quentin, as if unable to contain himself, broke in savagely, 'I can't understand why my father never mentioned
this to anyone else.'

'Leo probably swore him to silence, we'll never know,'
Charles sighed. 'Remember, Quentin, your father was
growing very absentminded. He was absorbed with his
wild life and horses. Most of the time he probably didn't
even remember Leo was there.'

'So you'll be taking Gina away from us?' Mrs Hurst
said regretfully.

'I hope so,' Charles replied dryly, adding almost angrily, 'You can't expect me to leave my only grandchild,
my heir, here, to continue working as a servant, Lydia? I
shall take her at once, and if what she's wearing is a
sample of the clothes she owns, I won't even wait for her
to pack. She can leave the rest behind and get rid of what
she has on, as soon as we find something else.'

Gina felt the nerves of her stomach tighten with apprehension. Suddenly she felt terribly afraid. She didn't
doubt Sir Charles had been telling her the truth, but he
was still a stranger. How could they expect her to get up
and just walk away with him? Tearfully she stared at
Quentin, but this time he made no attempt to come to
her aid. He simply stared back at her stonily, with what
was suspiciously like indifference in his eyes.

Wounded terribly by his lack of understanding, she

turned, as a desperate resort, to Mrs Hurst. 'Shouldn't I wait until you find someone to replace me? You've been so kind to me, I can't let you down.'

'No, dear,' gratified, Mrs Hurst smiled, 'you must go with your grandfather, I'm afraid. Your story has quite taken my breath away and I'm going to miss you, but he won't ever forgive me if I try to keep you. You can always come back to see us, you know,' she added rather anxiously, as Gina's face grew whiter.

Gina didn't listen. Distraught, she lost control and, without looking at her grandfather, hurled herself tearfully into Quentin's arms. 'I don't want to go, you have to save me! I belong to you,' she cried wildly.

'Don't be such a little fool, Gina. Pull yourself together.' His arms closed about her shaking body, momentarily she felt his hands gripping her trembling flesh, but not tenderly, and his angry breath thickening on her face. 'There's nothing here for you now.'

'So you keep telling me.'

'Then behave yourself!'

His hands still gripped her and she saw his face was grey as he stared down at her. 'I love you, Quentin,' she whispered, 'but you don't want me.'

'For heaven's sake, Gina, must you dramatise everything?' He sounded as though he couldn't take much more. 'Of course we want you,' he said curtly, 'but your place isn't here any more.'

While he still held her, he was fed up, she could tell. Fed up and indifferent as to what was to happen to her. A sudden hate stiffening her backbone, she wrenched herself from his arms. 'One day, Quentin Hurst, I'll show you!' she cried passionately. Then, without another word, well aware she was acting unforgivably, she turned and almost ran from the room. She wasn't to know, as she left Quentin that day, that it would be a whole year before she saw him again.

In spite of what she owned had been a childish display of temper, she hadn't wanted to leave Briarly. She had felt, irrationally, that she ought to have been given time to think it over. Sir Charles might have been an old family friend with an impeccable reputation, but it seemed to Gina that Quentin had got rid of her as quickly as he could. He was glad to see the last of her. The expression on his face as they had left had been grim, expressing not one flicker of regret.

While other girls might have been filled with elation at the prospect of such a brilliant future, all she could think of was Quentin and the way he had treated her, especially since her father died. Most of the time she might have been dirt under his feet. One day, she vowed bitterly, if she ever got the chance, she would treat him like dirt under hers!

Trying desperately to stop trembling, she had sat silently beside her grandfather in his beautiful Rolls. They had driven quickly away from Briarly, after he had exchanged a last private word with Quentin, with whom, she was surprised to see, he was still on the best of terms. She regretted, along with everything else, not having been given the opportunity of saying goodbye to Mrs Worth and the girls. She had even felt terrible over Matthews and kept recalling the startled look on his usually bland features as he had watched her departure.

Charles Hearn, being a man of rare understanding, didn't say very much until they reached the beautiful old period house where he lived. Quietly, after introducing Gina to his housekeeper, he ushered her into the drawing-room, a room just as magnificent as anything at Briarly. The housekeeper retired, saying she would bring them tea.

As they sat down, Charles said gently, with a sympathetic glance at her distressed young face, 'I realise this has been almost too much for you, dear, but you have absolutely nothing to fear. I know you feel it's all happened too quickly, but perhaps it's the best way. However, you must take your time, look on me as a new friend, if you like. Then you might learn to love me. But, whatever happens, I don't want you worrying about anything. Try to trust us, then I'm sure you'll begin to feel better.'

'Us?' Gina gazed at him nervously.

'My sister and I,' he smiled kindly. 'I expect she must be your great-aunt. I've decided it might be a good idea if we left immediately for London. I have another house there and your aunt lives with me. She always prefers London to the country, but then she's younger than I am—still in her fifties, a positive bundle of energy. If I know Liza she'll soon have you fixed up with everything you need. Then I think we'll travel—the three of us. How would you like that?' he asked with gentle eagerness. 'I've relations and friends all over the world. I love to travel, and I'm sure you will, once you've tried it. It will finish your education and help you to forget the past, and Briarly.'

CHAPTER FIVE

GINA, knowing Sir Charles was trying to give her time to adjust as much as anything else, didn't take what he was telling her too seriously. He was talking to her like a man walking extremely cautiously over thin ice. He was setting up pictures of a wonderful future as if intent on counteracting any possible side effects of shock, but at the moment all she longed for was complete assurance that Sir Charles really was her grandfather. Both he and Quentin had appeared to take it for granted that she would immediately believe it, but she had to have more proof. Instead of finding it easier to believe, as full realisation began to hit her, it was becoming all the more difficult.

After Mrs Bexley had brought their tea and left, Gina looked at Charles Hearn anxiously. Bluntly she asked. 'How can you be sure you aren't making a mistake? How can you be certain I really am your granddaughter? You're being very kind, but wouldn't it be terrible for both of us if you discovered at some future date that I wasn't the right girl?'

'But you are the right girl, Gina,' he smiled. Then his smile faded as he noticed the strained uncertainty of her expression. 'There's no doubt about it, child, as I've already told you. If it hadn't been true you can be sure Quentin Hurst would never have let you go. As it was I had a struggle, and I still can't decide whether the outcome pleased or angered him. However, as the facts were indisputable there was nothing he could do about it.'

So when it came to the crunch, Quentin had wanted to hang on to her. She might be impossible to replace—his mother's cheap slave. 'But how can he know anything about it?' she protested.

Charles glanced at her dryly. 'The two of us, Quentin and I, haven't spent most of the last few days with our respective lawyers for nothing. If there had been one loop-hole, one shred of doubt, we should have found it. Quentin went through everything with a fine tooth-comb, making absolutely sure we are related.'

'That I wasn't an impostor, more like it!' Gina retorted bitterly. He had called her plenty of awful things, what would be one more?

Charles said very soberly, 'I didn't stop to wonder whether it was on your behalf or mine, but I'm sure you have the wrong impression. I do know I shouldn't like to have him working against me. It wasn't until every detail was checked out that he gave me permission to approach you.'

Gina was startled, and indignant. 'You really had to ask for that?'

'Well, he seemed to have set himself up as your guardian, young lady, or at least as a man guarding your interests.'

'His mother's, no doubt,' she said shortly, then, some-what irrelevantly, 'I believe he's thinking of marrying Blanche Edgar. Do you know her?'

Charles nodded, slightly confused. 'Yes. Is it definite?'

'Well . . .'

'Gina,' he chided gently, his eyes shrewd on her slightly flushed face, 'I think it might be better if you forgot Quentin Hurst and Briarly for a while. When we come back you might like him better. I can only say that, as a man, I have an enormous respect for him, and he's been a great help in restoring you to me. As for marrying Blan-che Edgar—well, I'll believe it when I see it. I think he enjoys his freedom too much to give it up for any woman.'

Feeling strangely more comforted by this than by what

seemed absolute confirmation that she was Charles Hearn's granddaughter, Gina said stiffly, 'I hope I don't disappoint you.' Again recalling some of Quentin's insulting comments, she exclaimed, 'I'm afraid I'm very plain.'

'Of course you're not!' Charles returned sharply. 'It's merely those dreadful clothes you're wearing. If only,' he added grimly, 'I'd known where you were! I'm not sure that I'll ever be able to forgive your father for keeping you from me all these years, but there seems little point in animosity now.'

Gina watched him nervously, and, as if aware of her reluctance to talk to him about her father yet, he went on to tell her something about her mother. It was then that Gina sensed that a vital part of Charles Hearn had died with his daughter. He was only in his sixties, certainly he didn't appear old, but there was a sadness in his eyes when he spoke of her mother that made Gina soften towards him for the first time. It was clear that, in spite of his wealth, he had known a sorrow and unhappiness which more than matched her own.

Suddenly she found her attitude changing. She found herself hoping she might be able to make up a little for what he had lost. And, while she still felt they were more or less strangers, she knew she had taken the first step towards reconciling herself to the future.

There followed the most disturbing and exciting year, so far, in Gina's life. She was reluctant to leave the gentle Surrey countryside, but once in London she was immediately involved in a whirl of activity that left her little time to fret. Her great-aunt Liza instantly took her in hand, but so tactfully and pleasantly that afterwards Gina suspected she had learnt to love her even before she loved her grandfather.

Liza Cunningham, a childless widow, was in her element. Gina was taken to the best salons, where she was groomed and dressed until she felt she in no way resembled the girl who had lived at Briarly. Her red hair began looking truly wonderful, as did her face and figure, glowing with health and vitality. In Paris, a few weeks later, when a leading couturier said her figure was something to rave about, she still felt slightly incredulous. Yet sometimes, when she looked in the mirror before going out in the evenings, she did find it difficult to recognise herself and she often wondered what Quentin would think of her now. Sometimes if it occurred to her that she concentrated on improving herself solely with Quentin and revenge in mind, she dismissed such thoughts as absurd. It was because of her grandfather and Aunt Liza, no one else.

She got used to Rolls-Royces, houses in Mayfair, French chefs, Renoirs and Corots. Now she ate smoked salmon and pheasant, drank the best wines and grew knowledgeable about the latest thing in cocktails, even though she liked few of them. She had mink, dresses with famous Paris labels, jewellery from some of the great jewellers in the Place Vendome, perfume by Jean Patou, Balmain and Balenciaga, to name but a few.

When she protested to her aunt that her grandfather was spending far too much on her and that it wasn't necessary, Liza reproved her kindly.

'I shouldn't say a word, darling, if I were you. Your grandfather's a very wealthy man and you're all he has, and it's years since he's been this extravagant. Let him enjoy himself, it can't do any harm, and he might not have so many years left. Apart from that, you're almost bound to marry,' her eyes rested teasingly on Gina's glossy new beauty, 'and then he won't be so important in your life any more. So why not allow him to spoil you for the next few months, maybe a little longer if the right man doesn't come along?'

While often Gina longed to be back at Briarly, it wouldn't have been true to say that she didn't like living with these two people who loved her. It was all new and she would have been less than human if she hadn't enjoyed it. They left London and toured the world, visiting, as Charles had promised, friends and relations. They stayed at beautiful resorts in the Rockies, in skyscrapers in New York, a fourteenth-century castle in Spain, glass-sided penthouses in Rome, as well as many other places. In France there was a wonderful old chateau in the Dordogne, but one of her favourite places was a cousin's flat in Paris.

Louis was a cousin several times removed, but Gina felt an immediate kinship with him. He spoke impeccable English, but he made her speak French with him until she became quite fluent. He was older than she was and very sophisticated, but he had a good sense of humour and she enjoyed his company.

His flat, like many Paris houses, was set in a courtyard behind enormous wooden doors, and from it he showed her most of Paris while the older people rested. They had such fun together that Gina was convinced she had at last managed to forget Briarly and Quentin. Until Louis took her to the races at Longchamps, one day, and she saw a horse that reminded her too closely of Hector.

After this, in spite of a further few weeks spent sailing in the South of France on a fabulous yacht in fabulous weather, all she really craved for was to return home. She realised, at last, that the only way to get rid of the ghost of Quentin Hurst was to see him again. This hold he seemed to have over her, which no amount of idle flirting with other men seemed able to eliminate, was making her very bitter indeed. This, coupled with the way he had treated her, made her determined that, once back, she wouldn't seek to merely exorcise his ghost. She would, if it were at all possible, have some sort of revenge.

She had seen photographs of him from time to time with other women, but he had made no attempt to get in touch. So far as she knew he had never once enquired, since she had left Briarly, as to whether she were dead or alive. Once, in a bitter mood, she had thought of writing and asking how he was, but her good sense had prevailed. If he wasn't concerned for her, why should she worry over him? And she did see photographs!

While she didn't enjoy seeing photographs of him with other women, this made her feel fairly certain he wasn't yet married to Blanche. When they were in Rome, and she inadvertently learnt that he was also there, Gina had toyed with the idea of letting him know where she was staying. She had even got as far as deciding to consult her grandfather on the best way to reach him, when Sir Charles dropped the morning paper in her lap.

'I see our friend Quentin Hurst was enjoying himself last night.'

There had been a small photograph of him, dancing with a beautiful Italian girl. Gina had stared at it for a long time, then forgot about trying to contact him.

It was almost a year before they returned home, and, as they left London for Dorking, Gina knew that never, during all the time they had been away, had she ever been in such a state of intense excitement. By now she had learnt to love both her aunt and grandfather, a love not unmixed with gratitude for all they had done for her. Sitting between them, as they left the city, she felt entirely secure. Yet it was on Quentin Hurst that her mind concentrated. Charles and Liza were the safe, loving background. Quentin, who she was aware was none of these things, occupied her thoughts entirely.

While she hated to think she might react badly on meeting him again, she wanted to meet him as soon as possible. And when they did meet, she wanted to make as great an impact as possible—which ruled out her original plan to drive over and see him as soon as she got back. She knew Quentin. If she arrived on his doorstep wearing a simple little suit, he might never bother to look at her again. No, it would have to be a small after-dinner party here and one of her Paris models, with her hair freshly shampooed—for then it looked particularly glorious, and her face expertly made up—the lot! Otherwise she could well be wasting her time.

As they neared Dorking and her grandfather's estate, she asked tentatively, 'Do you think we could invite a few people in for drinks tomorrow evening, after dinner?'

'What a lovely idea!' Aunt Liza agreed at once, for she loved entertaining and felt happy that Gina wanted to be sociable.

Charles, knowing better than Liza did the kind of life Gina had led before he found her, hesitated. Gina, aware of it, glanced at him uncertainly. 'Grandfather?'

'You can ask whom you like, of course,' he assured her carefully. 'This is your home now, but why not wait a few days?'

'I'd like it to be tomorrow,' she insisted, with a stubbornness she could see surprised him. 'If it's all right with you?'

'It's not that,' his eyes narrowed slightly as he glanced at her sideways. 'Was there anyone in particular you wanted to ask?'

She lowered her thick lashes so he shouldn't see her agitation, forgetting the betraying pink in her cheeks. 'Not especially. There's Richard Hedley, if he's still around. He was the vet who used to come to Briarly to see the horses. Felix Duke was nice to me, too. And then there are the Hursts.'

'That's just four,' said Aunt Liza.

'Yes, well,' Gina hedged awkwardly, 'I'll have to leave the rest to you,' she bent her bright head. 'I didn't have many friends.'

'And now you would like more?' Liza thought she understood. 'Well, that should be easily arranged. How many?'

'How many? Oh, I see,' for a moment Gina felt bewildered, 'you mean for the party? Well, not too many. Just enough so it doesn't seem too cosy—if you know what I mean.'

She could see they didn't, but as she didn't know how to explain she lapsed into silence while the other two began discussing who should be invited. Liza didn't need pencil and paper; she was quite capable of handling a list of suitable guests in her head.

By the time they reached Bourne Court it was all settled and Gina thanked them. Once inside, another discussion began as to which bedroom she should be given. In the end it was decided she should have one at the very end of the first floor corridor, one which got both the morning and afternoon sun and had its own bathroom.

Gina, willing to agree to anything, escaped upstairs while Liza went to consult with Mrs Bexley over tomorrow's entertainment before she began ringing people. Gina felt rather guilty about the extra work, but Liza was in her element, as usual. Laughing, she promised to have her breakfast in bed, next morning, if she was at all tired.

At dinner, later that evening, she told them that nearly everyone had accepted.

Charles smiled wryly. 'They're probably all wondering why we should want to see them so soon.'

'We've been away almost a year, Charles,' his sister reproved him, 'and I suspect nearly everyone's curious about Gina.'

'What about the Hursts?' Charles asked the question which had been burning the tip of Gina's tongue.

'Quentin isn't at home,' Liza replied, 'but Lydia promised she would try and get hold of him. She's sure, if she can, he'll come. She won't be able to manage herself, as she has arranged to go away for a few days. She sends her regards, though, Gina, and hopes to see you soon.'

Most of the next day, apart from when she had her hair done, Gina spent with her grandfather, being shown over her new home. She thought it was beautiful but found it difficult to believe it would all be hers one day. This diffidence was something she knew she must try and overcome. She had looks and more beautiful clothes than

she knew what to do with. On top of this she was an
heiress with a titled grandfather. Yet underneath the
veneer of gloss and sophistication she had acquired over
the past year, she was still the less than confident young
girl she had once been. There was still a feeling of in-
feriority she was finding impossible to get rid of. For this
she continued to blame Quentin Hurst and was full of
resentment towards him because of it.

After dinner she went to change again into another
dress, teasing her grandfather, saying she must do him
justice. But when she emerged an hour later, Liza gave a
kind of startled gasp as she came to see what Gina was
doing and met her outside her bedroom door.

'Good heavens, child, someone's going to lose their eye-
sight,' she exclaimed. 'I can see Charles having to chase
hordes of young men away!'

Gina's laughter was gay but oddly strained. 'Truthfully, Aunt Liza, do you think I look much different from
the way I looked when you first saw me?'

Liza Cunningham's smile held pride. 'Vastly different,
my darling. In fact I'm willing to bet that few of the
people who knew you before will recognise you.'

Gratefully, Gina gave her aunt a quick hug. 'You go
down,' she begged, 'I forgot something. I'll follow in a
minute.'

She had only forgotten her courage. She tried to tell
herself it was because she couldn't bear to face a crowd of
curious people, but she knew that, for her, the crowd
would consist only of Quentin.

Cars were arriving and she couldn't put it off any
longer, but she need not have worried. Everyone made a
great fuss of her when she went downstairs, but Quentin
wasn't there. If he was coming he hadn't arrived yet, and
the relief she knew was wonderful. So wonderful that she
couldn't understand why she should feel impelled to seek
Liza out and suggest she should give him a ring.

Liza was too busy to take much notice. Absently she

shook her beautifully waved head. 'Better wait a little longer, dear. He'll probably be here in a minute.'

He was. As Gina stood chatting to Richard Hedley, Quentin came through the door of the big lounge which was crowded with people. She saw him speak to her grandfather, who went to meet him, then his dark eyes were searching the room, seeking and finding her.

He hadn't changed, she was the one who had done that, and she sensed, even with the width of the room between them, that he was immediately conscious of it. Her heart jerked and began racing in the old familiar way, his name coming inaudibly to her lips as in a dream, while the only sane part of her functioning commanded she pull herself together. If she played her cards right, that same voice whispered, he might soon be eating out of her hand.

It took a lot of effort, but she managed to smile at him brightly. She couldn't be absolutely sure that she held his whole attention, but it seemed like it. For the moment it was sufficient to see interest flaring as his gaze pinned hers, as, without once removing his eyes from her face, he wended his way towards her through the crowd. Without being aware of it, she left Richard's side and moved towards him, so she could be alone with him when they met. They might have been quite alone for all the notice either of them took of anyone else.

'Gina!' To her surprise he bent to kiss her cheek, putting his hands on her arms to do so.

To her dismay, her racing heart drove the colour from her cheeks when he touched her, but deliberately she attempted to hide her feelings. 'Hello, Quentin,' she smiled at him again, this time more seductively, as she had seen other girls doing on her travels. Her smile widened to a teasing grin. 'Or do I say Mr Quentin?'

Just for a second his eyes narrowed, but to her relief he decided to accept the smile and ignore the dig. Something warned her she must learn not to betray her resentment, for, even cloaked in a smile, he might guess it was still there.

'Well, well! Quite a transformation!' He made no attempt to disguise his appreciation, as his eyes went closely over her—and he did this as if he had every right. The tight black dress wasn't her favourite, but it served its purpose, being designed to draw the attention of even the least observant to the perfect lines of her figure. She wasn't fond of black, but the colour did seem to do a lot for her white skin and flaming red hair, which curled down her back in a blaze of glory.

Quentin was taking his time, inspecting her, and she felt strangely breathless as his gaze passed slowly across her smooth, unblemished face, pausing on the full curve of her lips before plunging hungrily with her dress to the enticing roundness of her breasts. Insolence joined the appreciation in his eyes, enough to make her quiver, although she gave no visible sign of it.

'So now,' he said coolly, 'you're grown up? You've learnt how to dress, to—er—make——' she was sure he had been going to say show, 'the most of yourself?'

'Are you paying me a compliment?' she asked sharply.

'Aren't you sure?' he challenged mockingly.

'You never did—in the past,' she retorted.

'Ah, but you've left the past behind you, haven't you?' he drawled. 'The girl I knew wasn't interested in herself, only horses.'

'Naturally,' she allowed coolly, 'I've changed.'

'You've learnt how to make the most of yourself, anyway,' he mused, his glance mocking. 'Do you always wear your hair loose like that, like a flaming banner?'

'Don't you think it looks nice?'

'Answer my question first, Gina.'

'Oh, all right,' she blurted, with a sudden, irrational desire to shock him, 'I like it this way because it's sexy and free.'

He merely laughed, as if her answer amused him. 'And

do you actually feel sexy and free, eager to indulge your-self?'

'Now you're twisting my words.'

'Not necessarily.' His face, even more good-looking than she seemed to remember, hardened. 'From the first moment you saw me tonight, you've been throwing out some kind of challenge, and I'm curious.'

She flushed, her glance wavering from his dark, intensely masculine one. 'Wouldn't I know better than to throw anything in your direction?'

'I don't know,' he paused reflectively. 'You've certainly changed. You were always sharply intelligent and I can see you've picked up quite a lot while you've been away. If you haven't actually practised all you've learnt, I should think you know, or imagine you know, how to go about it. Once we were poles apart in experience, but the gap might be nothing now.'

Irritated beyond measure by a wave of embarrassment, Gina snapped, 'Why should you doubt I haven't slept with a man?'

'No reason why I should,' he agreed, with a faint hint of violence. 'I might even be pleased to hear you had. Before you left Briarly you were extremely young and innocent.'

'Before I left Briarly,' she retorted bitterly, 'I was very innocent about a lot of things.'

'But not now?'

He was going too fast for her. They had met, but weren't having the sensible kind of conversation she had envisaged, after not seeing each other for so long. Their voices were racing, yet they hadn't even touched on health, their respective families, the weather, all the normal things. She seemed to have been plunged immediately into waters too deep to swim in.

Staring at him, she was aware that her deepening colour must be defeating her efforts to appear more sophisticated than she actually was. And she hated to think she was giving him a chance of amusing himself at her expense. He possessed a sexy, animal-like magnetism, controlled though it might be, which she had never been so completely conscious of before. In vain she tried to remember clearly how she had felt a year ago when he had kissed her, yet this didn't stop her from wondering how she would feel if he should kiss her again. He attracted her, as she supposed he must attract many women, and every instinct warned her to flee.

Inwardly she despaired of her own cowardly tremors. Why should she run from Quentin Hurst? He still attracted her, but she was older now, well able to fight him—or to play with a little fire without getting burnt. Old enough, surely, to be able to appreciate an attractive man without falling head over heels in love with him. Frowning, her eyes lingered on the steely strength of his fine, well cared for hands, which lightly gripped his glass of whisky. His cuffs were immaculate and there was a dark sprinkling of hairs on his wrist. Suddenly all her confidence left her.

Wishing, too late, that she had dressed in something different, she exclaimed jerkily, 'You don't think I look young and innocent any more?'

His smile was derisive, really an answer in itself. 'You still look young, and you're beautiful, but I don't know about innocent. Are you?'

'Nothing like being blunt, is there?' she tossed at him. 'Do you really care? What would you like me to say?'

He laughed. 'Suppose you say nothing. Let me find out for myself. I like mystery.'

'Only if you're able to solve it?'

'Eventually. Anything wrong with that?'

Her eyes flashed at his arrogance. 'Most men, I believe, lose interest at that stage.'

'Try me?' he said, so softly teasing that she blushed.

'I'd be a fool if I had anything to do with you,' she sighed.

'You don't sound convinced.'

'There's Blanche.'

'No Blanche.'

Excitement stirred within her, her heart beginning to beat faster, as his hand curved shamelessly over her bare arm, like a caress. Then her grandfather was there, asking Quentin proudly what he thought of Gina now. Listening to his amusingly flattering reply, Gina realised he knew all the answers, but then he was no gauche youth to be stammering under Charles's steely regard. He had charm, a very potent kind of charm which, in spite of her former bravado, might be better left alone.

After a few minutes she murmured an excuse and turned away.

He caught her up. 'Why don't you come with me and see Hector. I still have him.'

'What, now?'

'I can see he means more to you than I do,' correctly he interpreted the brightening of her eyes. 'Go and put a coat on. For my peace of mind, not the cold,' he grinned, for the night was warm. 'I'll make your excuses. Most people are leaving, anyway.'

'I'd rather not.'

His face darkened. 'You'll do as I say.'

The cheek of him! Just as he used to be! How could he expect her to desert her party just like that?

'Refuse and I'll drag you out.'

'You're starting as you mean to go on?'

'Yes, you bad-tempered little redhead!' Quentin took no notice of her sarcastic tones as he pushed her out of the room towards the stairs. 'I'll meet you at the back door in exactly three minutes, then everyone will think this has all been too much for you and you've gone to bed.'

Gone to bed, indeed! She wanted to refuse, but Quentin and Hector, together, proved too tempting a combination. It was still early and there was nothing else to do but go to bed. Inside her was an irresistible longing to see Briarly again, which she suspected Quentin had astutely guessed. She had been homesick for it for a long, long time.

All the same, not wishing to give Quentin the impression that she couldn't wait, she sat silently beside him, not speaking until they were there.

'What's wrong?' He spoke sharply, as they turned into the drive at Briarly, leaving the main road.

'I don't know. Perhaps it's too soon to come back?'

'Ruthless therapy can be best.'

'You think I'm in need of—therapy? You believe there's something I should get out of my system?'

'Quite a lot, as a matter of fact.'

Gina slanted a smouldering glance at the hard line of his jaw. 'For whose convenience, I wonder?'

His mouth quirked. 'You could make a start on all that resentment.'

Hating his shrewdness, she deliberately chose to misunderstand. 'It wasn't nice to drag me away from my first party.'

'But then you never considered me a very nice person,' he retorted indifferently. 'You're already convinced I'm not.'

It had to slip out. 'You did your best to convince me, when I worked here.'

'You don't work for me now.'

So he didn't intend to discuss it. 'I'm only beginning to realise the difference this is going to make,' she rejoined smartly.

'When I asked you here tonight, it wasn't a licence to say what you like,' he said suavely, 'so be careful.'

'You don't change, do you?' she muttered sullenly, as they drew up outside the house.

'Maybe it's just as well.' He switched off the engine smoothly. 'I believe you've been subject to too much change in the past year. Your grandfather meant well, but it's left you as mixed up as ever.'

'How?'

'Once you were frightened of the past, now it's the future,' he returned cryptically, as he drew her from the car and steered her gently towards the stables, his hand on her arm no less possessive than it had been in her grandfather's house.

It was like going back in time, and she felt a lump in her throat. Everything was in the right place—the house, the trees with their wavering shadows, the gardens, the huge old stone buildings behind them. Even the woods were still there, Quentin mustn't have had them cut down. With a slight shiver Gina wondered about the cottage, but she didn't ask. She couldn't plunge back into the past too quickly.

She confined her curiosity to less important things. 'Do you have the same groom?'

'Yes.'

'And your mother, did she find another girl?'

'Eventually. But she's middle-aged, rather than young, and she's having a few days off while my mother is away.'

Quentin opened the stable door for her and for a guilty instant she wondered if anyone had ever found the key she had hidden among her belongings. Possibly someone had returned it to him when her things had been cleared out.

To her delight Hector recognised her. 'At least I think he does!' she exclaimed as she hugged him, turning a suddenly radiant face towards Quentin.

'While I'm relieved to see that something about Briarly still pleases you, it's not doing your fur coat any good,' he pointed out dryly.

Flushing, she drew back. 'I suppose you're referring to my old habits? You were forever telling me I looked untidy.'

He frowned, then smiled mildly. 'And you were always too sensitive, guaranteed to react. Let's go back to the house for some coffee.'

She didn't argue, although she felt she should have gone straight back to Bourne Court. It was getting late, but she seemed unable to resist any suggestion made by Quentin this evening. Besides, she was curious.

'Do you realise,' she said coolly, 'it's the first time I've been here as a guest?'

'Must you constantly harp back to the past?' he asked impatiently.

'No,' she replied, wondering how he could expect her to forget it. Surely he didn't suppose she could wipe out almost eighteen years of her life. She recalled how he used to treat her, his brutal, often callous remarks. If he had never actually hurt her physically, he had wounded her feelings time and time again. And now he asked her to forget it! No—he expected her to forget it. Fretfully she sighed, owning that it might be wiser to, and childish not to. Yet it was difficult not to remember that while all she had craved was a little sympathy and understanding, all she had received was cruel indifference. For one kind word from him, then, she would have given anything. Now, when it appeared he was ready to bestow much more than kindness, she wasn't sure if she wanted anything from him at all.

'Is Matthews still here?' As they went through to the drawing-room, she looked about her.

'He is, but I told him not to wait up.'

'Nothing's changed.'

'Not even you, only your looks, so don't sound so tragic.' Quentin began filling coffee cups from a hot flask, his hands steady, his voice clipped. 'How do you like it? Black or white?'

It seemed another indication of past neglect that he didn't know. 'White,' she said tonelessly.

His grey eyes flickered and his mouth tightened, as if he restrained another curt retort. Lifting a mocking eyebrow, he passed her her coffee. 'How do you like being an heiress?' he asked, changing the subject.

'I'm not sure . . .' Eagerly she turned to him, as she had often done in the old days, when she had quickly forgotten each new grievance. 'I'm not sure how I feel, Quentin. Not much different, I'm afraid.'

'Why afraid?' He moved his dark head slightly back to look at her. 'Did you expect to be different almost overnight?'

A sigh left her lips as she stared down at her coffee. 'I've been away over a year.'

'I know.'

Did his grimness mean he wished she hadn't come back? 'I've seen a lot of places. I've met men . . .'

'Many?'

'Quite a few,' she tried to be truthful. 'I liked a distant cousin in Paris very much, but his friends were very sophisticated.' She glanced up with a wry smile, meeting Quentin's narrowed eyes. 'I tried to be like them, but I don't know if I succeeded.'

He laughed. Coming across to her, he drew her slowly to her feet, placing her empty cup to one side. 'If I were you, Gina, I'd forget about the year you've been away. I can't see any problems. You're young and beautiful and grown up at last. Why not forget about all these other men you've met and concentrate solely on me?'

CHAPTER SIX

GASPING a little at his audacity, Gina felt her heartbeats quicken as Quentin pulled her closer. Why was he asking such things of her? He certainly had no right to any of her time, never mind all of it. As for suggesting she should concentrate on him, he would soon tire of her if she did.

'Why the sudden change of heart?' She asked coolly. 'You never noticed me before, or showed any great desire for my company.'

'You never looked as you do now, before,' he said huskily. 'Outwardly you aren't the same girl, inwardly I hope you haven't changed too much. When you lived here we didn't always agree, but the few times I had you in my arms I didn't want to let you go. You must have known that.'

'All I remember was you couldn't push me away quick enough.'

'I thought I frightened you?'

'Yes,' her green eyes widened with a sense of injury, 'you did.'

'Try a little harder,' he taunted. 'You felt something, I'm certain.'

'If I did,' she lied, 'I can't recall it.'

'You need reminding?'

Before she could escape he lowered his head, tilting up her rounded chin at the same time. Firmly his mouth came down over hers as she stared irresolutely up at him. His mouth was cool but possessive, quite unyielding. Bewildered, Gina closed her eyes, but not before she had seen the grey of his turn almost to black.

As his lips touched hers she felt a rush of sensation that

immediately took her back to the night of the storm by
the lake, only this was a storm of a different kind. This
one dredged up memories, tossing them at her, ruthlessly
whirling the past into the present until she knew the
months between might never have been.

Quentin had relieved her of her coat in the hall and
the black dress proved no obstacle to his searching hands.
As the pressure of his mouth deepened and reality faded,
she felt him pushing the silky material from her shoulders
and his hands closing over her taut breasts. She could feel
the strength of his fingers, their tight grip on her warm
skin and gave an inarticulate little moan, her lips parting
helplessly under his as passion rose hotly between them.

'Please don't,' she whispered, shivering in his grasp as
his mouth left hers to slowly follow the direction of his
hands, trailing sensuously over her, until she cried out.

Her protest must have been a mistake. It brought his
head up, but his lips hardened as he began kissing her
mouth again, not apparently caring if he hurt her. Gina
had a curious feeling of floating helplessly in space.
Wildly she found herself clutching Quentin's broad shoulders, as if to keep from falling, as a shaft of piercing,
lightning-like sensation rendered her limbs incapable of
supporting her.

Then, as though he considered he had inflicted sufficient punishment, he ended the kiss with a mutter of satisfaction, staring down at the light perspiration on her face.
'That night by the lake,' he said thickly, 'I almost made
love to you.'

Her voice croaked. 'You did.'

'Not properly, but you were a great temptation. I
could never remember wanting anything so much. You
were so small, yet your body fitted into mine perfectly, if
not just quite near enough. You're still small and beautifully made, and when I kiss you I find I want you as
much as ever.'

'For heaven's sake!' She was trembling, but made herself exclaim, 'Do we have to be so dramatic? What's a kiss?'

Tightly he replied, as if her flippancy didn't please him, 'I can't answer that, not now. I thought I knew.'

Her heart jerked at his grimness, but she drew back, refusing to weaken. 'You've spoilt a pleasant evening.'

'Spoiled?' His face reddened slightly, and Gina was pleased she could get under his skin. It gave her a faint sense of power. Suddenly, the thoughts of revenge that had persisted vaguely at the back of her mind didn't seem so impossible any more. On the other hand, Quentin too might be seeking revenge for the bother she had caused him while he had been forced to employ her. His kisses had the flavour of it; certainly they had held little tenderness.

'I've got used to a more refined approach,' she returned his gaze frostily, as she adjusted her dress with shaking fingers, not telling him he was the first, the only man, she had allowed to touch her so intimately. 'You still feel you own me, Quentin.'

'I intend to,' he rasped harshly, his eyes glittering. 'And before anyone else gets in.'

'Like you do in business?'

'You nasty little bitch!'

'I can see why you're still unmarried, if that's a sample of the endearments you use!' Her green eyes darkened scornfully. 'I'd like to go home, please.'

'It might be a good idea. I thought you'd grown up?'

'You thought I'd be ready to fall into your arms, have an affair with you.'

'You could do worse,' he drawled.

'That's a matter of opinion.' Again she felt she was being childish, but she couldn't fight Quentin on his own grounds. She was too inexperienced, both verbally and physically, to compete. So she could only stick to the kind of retort which seemed, at least, to make him angry. As he put her back in his car, she wondered if she would ever see him again, and was surprised, at Bourne Court, when he asked her to return next day to Briarly, to ride with him.

'Tomorrow's Saturday, so I'm not going to London. If you come about ten?'

Gina was startled yet strangely relieved. 'I'd like to,' she confessed honestly, 'but I think I should ask Grandfather and Aunt Liza first. They might have made other plans.'

'Gina,' Quentin looked down on her firmly, 'they've had you a whole year.'

'Oh,' she drew a deep breath as he searched her face, 'neither of them is that possessive. They like me to have friends, but we've just got—er—home,' why did she find it so difficult to call any place but Briarly home? Knowing a surge of resentment because of this, she added, 'And Grandfather might consider you're too old for me.'

Quentin didn't argue about this. 'Liza has already asked me to dine tomorrow, here, which must be a sign of approval. If I promise to bring you back after lunch I'm sure Charles won't protest too much.'

Gina bit her lip. His voice was dry and he was going too fast for her. While she wanted to go to Briarly she had no wish to be swept off her feet. 'I'm not sure,' she hesitated.

'Of course you are,' he grinned, taking her consent for granted, as with a casual wave he roared back down the road, without waiting for her reply.

Everyone had gone to bed, which increased her feelings of guilt. The clock in the hall was only chiming one as she went upstairs, but she still felt she ought to have been earlier. She hadn't intended staying out so long and blamed Quentin. She fell asleep thinking about him, arguing with herself that he was dangerous and better left alone, while her less sensible self whispered that there could be no harm in seeing him one more time.

When she came down to breakfast she apologised for

going out and for being late in. Then she asked if they would mind if she went riding with Quentin.

If anything her grandfather looked relieved, and Liza said it was all right by her, she was having coffee with a friend. 'Although I did half promise to bring you with me,' she glanced at Gina, teasing lightly. 'Rebecca was enchanted with you at the party last night and has an unmarried son.'

'It was a lovely party,' Gina smiled gratefully.

'You looked beautiful, we were very proud of you, weren't we?' Liza turned to Charles, who agreed.

'I have a lot to see to, this morning,' he said ruefully, after they had discussed the party a little more. 'Comes of being away so long, so it's just as well you've both got something to do.'

'Can't I stay and help?' Gina offered immediately, but he refused.

'Off you go and enjoy yourself,' he smiled. 'You're only young once and I'm sure you'll be safe with Quentin.'

How safe was she with Quentin? The question teased Gina all the way to Briarly, bringing with it alternate waves of apprehension and indignation mixed with excitement. No one but the two of them knew what had gone before. Quentin had been part of her life, part of her growing up, the man responsible for her somewhat abrupt transition from a young girl into a woman. Did he want now to take her further?

She recalled how he had kissed her when she had lived at Briarly. He had acted impulsively, his kiss evoked out of anger, but last night there had been something deliberate in his lovemaking which made her suspect this was the way he intended to go on. She attracted his senses now, more than his anger, and she didn't think he was a man who wholly denied himself in that direction.

As if he had been waiting for her, he came out of the house exactly as she arrived in the small car she had borrowed from Charles. She had passed her driving test in

London, after what she considered must have been the fastest course ever with a good instructor, but she hadn't yet a car of her own.

'The car and the girl don't match,' he smiled, opening the door for her.

Her pulse rate flicked to medium fast, but she managed to stay composed. 'They aren't meant to,' she shrugged.

'Well worn and practical,' he patted the car bonnet, 'while you're neither.'

'I'm not sure whether that's a compliment or an insult!' She pretended to look doubtful as she gazed at him.

It wasn't easy, in the face of Quentin's immediate impact, to carry on a light conversation. He was dressed, this morning, like herself, in casual jeans and a sweater, and she found it as difficult as she had done the previous evening to remove her eyes from his lean, well muscled figure.

'This is one of Grandfather's cars which he doesn't use very much,' she explained. 'He would like me to have one of my own, but I can't decide on the make. I don't know much about cars, but I suppose I'll have to make up my mind.'

'So what would you like? Something sporty?'

'I'm not sure,' she smiled wryly. 'I think I'm more interested in horses.'

His brows lifted. 'That's not news to me. You always have been.'

They made their way to the stables, after she had refused coffee. She had wanted to speak to Matthews and Mrs Worth, to say hello to the girls, but she supposed she would see them later.

They were mounted and away when she suddenly said, 'Grandfather has promised to get me a horse of my own as soon as possible, so I won't have to keep on coming here.'

'There's nothing to stop you.' Quentin's mouth tightened as he rode nearer her. 'A few minutes in a car. Why go to the expense?'

'It's something I've always wanted,' she protested, 'a horse of my own. You know it is.'

'I have four here, Gina. They're all yours.'

'No, seriously . . .'

'I am serious.' He caught hold of her reins, making her halt, his eyes fixed on the glowing beauty of her face, with a hint of irony.

'Let's go on.' She stirred restively, her saddle leather creaking, unwilling to argue with him about it.

'Not until I've talked to you.' He ignored the swiftly imploring glance she gave him. 'If you have a horse of your own, you have to look after it, or pay someone else to do it, and it's expensive.'

Her green eyes changed aloofly, as she sensed criticism. 'My grandfather can afford it, I believe.'

Quentin seemed to hesitate before asking dryly, 'Are you sure? He must have spent quite a lot this last year, perhaps more than he could afford.'

'Well, I don't believe that!'

His voice was curt. 'Forget I mentioned it.'

Gina returned primly, 'I think we both should. My grandfather is a wealthy man.'

'Don't boast about it too much.'

Hating his advice, which she knew in her heart was good, she replied sharply, 'Oh, I know it's not the thing to boast about money, but I can't see any sense in not mentioning it at all. At least it's freed me from you. I expect it annoys you to find you have no hold over me any more.'

Anger glittered in his eyes but went just as quickly. 'Power doesn't always lie in money, my dear.' As colour stained her cheeks, he smiled enigmatically, 'Suppose we return to discussing horses? If you really want one of your own, I could let you have Leonie, the mare you're riding. She's always liked you, and when you're in London she could stay here, while you're away.'

'Why should I want to go to London?' she hedged, curiously reluctant to do as he suggested. 'We've only just left it.'

'You'll want to go occasionálly, for different reasons. Shopping, getting your hair done—to see a show.'

'Will I?'

'Of course you will. Don't be awkward. You can stay at your grandfather's house or my apartment, if you're in London alone.'

'Your apartment?' she queried.

'Yes. It will be cónvenient when I take you out. When we feel like something more than the kind of entertainment to be found around here.'

'I'll think about it,' she said, hunching her shoulders as she used to do when she had trailed behind Quentin and his friends, when she had worked for him.

'Don't do that!'

Hearing his impatient exclamation, Gina jerked upright, also as she had used to do when he spoke to her sharply.

She flung him an angry glance. 'I'm not your servant now, so you can stop shouting at me and ordering me about!'

'I'm not shouting, or trying to order you around, but,' his voice darkened menacingly, 'if you mention that period of your life again, I'll not be responsible.'

'Oh, let's gallop,' she cried, suddenly jerking her reins away from him as he bent threateningly nearer. The smouldering expression in his eyes made her nerves leap uncontrollably, but she managed to laugh lightly over her shoulder, 'It's too nice a morning to quarrel.'

They returned to a late lunch, Quentin, she considered, having kept her out longer than he should have done. They had found a pub and rested the horses while they went inside and drank cool lager in the dark old taproom. They hadn't talked much but Quentin's eyes had dwelt on her almost continually, and he hadn't attempted to disguise the fact that she intrigued him, and he was finding her more and more attractive.

It was the same later, after dinner, when Sir Charles was called to the telephone and Liza was called away as well. Gina had hoped vaguely that something might prevent Quentin from coming, but he turned up promptly at seven.

'I can't get over your changed appearance,' from his seat beside her on a satin brocaded sofa, he spoke lazily as the door closed behind Liza. 'You're so small, slender and graceful, all I want to do is look at you.'

'You've been doing that for the last hour,' Gina retorted, her heart not unaffected by his close regard. 'How can I be sure it's not a smut on my nose attracting your attention? Or perhaps,' she resorted to the flippancy which seemed her only defence against him, 'it's simply my new immaculateness you find so fascinating?'

He laughed, while for a moment she thought he was about to berate her for mentioning the past after having warned her not to. Then he stopped laughing and enlightened her soberly, 'I have seen you since you left, you know.'

'You have?' The breath left her throat in a gasp, because she could scarcely believe it.

He frowned, noting her surprise. 'You didn't think I wouldn't have to reassure myself you were all right?'

'Your conscience?' Her face fell.

'Call it what you like,' he said curtly.

'I don't know anything more charitable, not where you're concerned.'

'Gina!' his curt tone didn't alter, 'stop trying to be smart, it doesn't suit you. Not as much as your dress does.' There was a faint mockery in his face as he made a conscious effort to lighten the conversation.

'This is quite modest!' Immediately suspicious, on re-calling his reactions to the little black dress she had worn at the party, she raised her eyes to him briefly, then just as quickly looked away. The concoction of frothy green chiffon she wore tonight was modest by comparison, but the colour flattered her skin and gave a wonderful sheen to her titian hair. She hadn't been aware of it until she saw the brief blaze in his grey eyes.

'Very modest in appearance,' he agreed ironically, 'if not in effect.' His eyes lingered broodingly on the smooth column of her throat before slipping further to where her skin gleamed palely through the vee of the fragile bodice. 'I've caught glimpses of you from time to time,' he con-fessed unexpectedly, 'but it didn't completely prepare me for the change in you.' His dark brows lifted slightly as her eyes widened. 'Did you ever think of me at all, Gina, while you were away? Or, what's probably more import-ant, how do you see me, now that you're back?'

'Much as I always did.' Agonisingly aware of him, she sought to conceal it under an indifferent shrug, refusing to confess he was the only man she ever really saw. This would give him power over her, and her new freedom wasn't to be sacrificed so lightly.

Suddenly he pulled her ruthlessly to him, as though determined to find more satisfactory answers another way. As they came stormily together, he bent his head, kissing her with a demanding intensity, his arms locked around her tightly. Once again Gina knew a surge of strange wild excitement, but terrified of what her lips might reveal, she resisted him stiffly.

Her resistance appeared to annoy him, turning a mild frustration into something tinged with violence. It only lasted a few moments, but when he released her, her mouth was bruised and sore, her whole body shaking, on fire. Only her voice was cold, and even that trembled.

'Is this some new form of the punishment you were always so good at dispensing?'

'I could smack you for that,' he said ominously. 'But if you think it's wrong to want someone, it proves you're still innocent. I could teach you a lot—if you were mine it would be easy.'

'Total possession? It seems to be a hobby of yours!' she retorted scornfully, trying to steady her voice. 'Once I saw you in Rome, with a lovely Italian countess, and you seemed to have that in mind.'

'You saw me?' His eyes narrowed in slight surprise.

'In a newspaper picture,' she confessed.

'I thought as much,' his smile was cruel. 'Photographs are notorious for giving the wrong impression. I've almost forgotten her name.'

'But she mightn't yours.'

Quentin shrugged his broad shoulders, but Charles and Liza were back, leaving Gina to guess what Quentin's answer might have been.

The next morning she rode and lunched with him again, and this became a routine which she found herself sticking to. Sometimes she came over early and they went out together before Quentin went off to London, but occasionally she went to Briarly later, deliberately to avoid seeing him. Yet when her grandfather proposed doing something definite about getting her her own horse, she put him off with an excuse, saying she hadn't made up her mind as to what she wanted.

She knew she was using Quentin's horses as an excuse for seeing so much of him, but, while feeling ashamed of herself, she couldn't resist the temptation. He was too much of a challenge, he aroused in her feelings which were hard to define but equally hard to ignore. Neither could she tell, on his part, whether it was conscience over the past or plans for the future that was driving him. She did know, though, that although he hadn't touched her again since the night he had dined at Bourne Court, the darkness of his eyes often made her shiver with a strange feeling of anticipation.

He was angry when she had dinner with Richard Hedley, and even more so when she went out with Felix Duke. She had been seeing quite a lot of Felix. It was remarkable, but each time she was riding alone he had a habit of appearing from nowhere. He took her back to his home for coffee and his mother was charming to her. Then twice he had asked her out for dinner and dancing and she had accepted. After the last occasion Quentin found out.

'Why go with him and not me?' he snapped.

'You never mentioned anything but London,' she replied, equally sharp.

'Which isn't a thousand miles away! I didn't press you because I thought you wanted time to settle down.'

'Who told you about Felix?' she asked, her heart beating unevenly at his anger.

'Never mind,' his voice chilled as he watched the colour flare under her soft, petal-like skin. 'It's true, I suppose?'

'Quentin!' her voice was faintly incredulous. 'You don't own me. I can go out with whom I like.'

'Of course you can,' he was utterly reasonable, 'but why break hearts? Duke happens to be in love with you, and you'll never love him.'

'How do you know?' She glared at him, hating the confident note in his voice so much that she added coldly, 'Do I have to be in love with a man before I go out with him?'

'In some cases, no,' he agreed tightly.

'Besides,' she looked away, 'it was something to do.'

'Why don't you get yourself a job if you're bored?'

'I could do.'

'No,' he hesitated, his voice still grim, 'I don't think it's such a good idea. It might be better if you came up to London for a few days. You could lunch with me and I'd take you out in the evenings. Charles and Liza won't mind, Liza might even care to come with you and leave Charles to get his year's absence sorted out in peace.'

It was tempting, not because Gina particularly wanted to go to London just now, but the thought of wining and dining and dancing with Quentin was too attractive to be denied. Yet she felt nervous of committing herself. She sensed he was attracted to a certain extent and while she had thought to use this attraction to punish him, each day her serious doubts that she could handle such a situation were growing. She might be safer here than in London, at present. It could be easier to retreat.

'Liza has an appointment at the end of the month,' she said, pretending his mention of Liza had reminded her. 'I think I'll wait until then. I'm only just beginning to get to know Bourne Court.'

If she had been quite honest she would have said she was more absorbed in renewing her acquaintance with Briarly. Quentin's mother had returned and she often had coffee with her in the mornings, after she had been out riding. Matthews, to Gina's secret amusement, couldn't do enough for her, but in spite of his former disapproval, she had always liked him and never reminded him of the days when he had scorned her. Mrs Worth and the girls also seemed dazzled by the new Gina, but she hoped they didn't believe she had changed all that much.

Mrs Hurst, while seeming appreciative of her changed appearance, was wary of her. Gina sensed this, yet was unable to guess why. Not until Blanche Edgar was mentioned, one day, did she recall how Mrs Hurst had once nursed certain hopes in that direction, and possibly, if mistakenly, considered Gina something of a threat.

'I think she would make Quentin an admirable wife,' Mrs Hurst smiled, when Gina asked frankly why she hadn't seen Blanche at Briarly since she had come back. Quentin had said nothing to her and she hadn't asked him, fearing he might think her jealous, especially after the way she had spoken of Blanche at Bourne Court.

'Doesn't Quentin think so, too?' She tried to keep her voice light.

His mother frowned uncertainly. 'He does seem extremely fond of her. I know he's been seeing quite a lot of her, but now that she's working in London I'm not so sure.'

'No Blanche!' he had stated, and so emphatically, as if she had no part in his life any more. Who did he think he was fooling? 'Perhaps they're just good friends,' she suggested sweetly.

'They did seem more than that,' Mrs Hurst sighed. 'I can't understand what's happened.'

Gina smiled and wished she didn't feel so sick. 'Blanche could have changed her mind. Why does she work in London?'

An expression of fleeting distaste crossed Mrs Hurst's face. 'Her father died and C.T.T. hit the family hard. Blanche had to find something. Her brother and his wife still carry on, but they're having a struggle.'

So Quentin hadn't been telling the whole truth about Blanche. He had used his deviousness to give the wrong impression. Gina was swamped by a wave of scorn. He must realise Blanche was in love with him and he went on seeing her, without having any intention, apparently, of marrying her. For surely if he had he would have asked her before now? She recalled how he used to take Blanche out—stroll with her in the gardens—take her riding. What had happened? Surely the worsening of Blanche's family fortunes hadn't influenced him? Quentin must have more than enough of his own.

One morning Quentin rang her early to tell her that as Jenkins, the groom, was taking a day or two off to attend to some personal matters, he wouldn't be there if she needed any assistance.

'I'd rather you stayed away until he gets back,' he said. 'I don't like you riding when there's no one around.'

'How do you think I used to manage?' she asked coolly, wriggling into the nightdress she had discarded during the night.

'What on earth are you doing?' he enquired tersely, as the line crackled and her voice faded. 'Gina! Are you still there?'

'I'm only putting my nightdress on before Betty arrives with my tea,' she choked unthinkingly, emerging suffocatingly from clouds of clinging silk.

'Don't you sleep in it?' He sounded faintly amused, yet his voice deepened in a way which sent her pulses suddenly racing.

'Not always.' She wished she hadn't mentioned it. 'I couldn't sleep last night, it was so hot.'

'Perhaps I could help there.'

The colour flamed in her cheeks so warmly, she was glad he couldn't see. He spoke so evenly, without a hint of innuendo, that he could easily have been thinking of hot milk.

Quickly she reverted to the stables, agreeing with apparent meekness, 'I might take your advice and not come over today. I do have other things to do.'

'Have you?' Quentin paused, and when she didn't reply, said, 'I wish I had nothing else to do but satisfy my curiosity. Unfortunately I have to fly to Paris this morning.'

'Will I see you later?' she asked, oddly breathless.

'You might,' he replied doubtfully, leaving her wondering whether he intended spending his evening in Paris, or with Blanche in London as he rang off.

When she got down to really thinking about it, Gina changed her mind about staying away from the stables, feeling quite excited at the unexpected chance of having them completely to herself. But as she had promised to go out with Liza that morning, she didn't get over to Briarly until after lunch.

There wasn't anything to do. As it was summer, Jenk-

ins had simply turned the horses out in the nearby pad-
dock, where they looked so content in the sunshine that
Gina changed her mind about going riding. It was after
three and she felt hot and a little tired from a morning
spent shopping with an indefatigable Liza, who had re-
lentlessly attempted to track down something which in
the end had proved unobtainable. She wouldn't have
bothered to come to Briarly today if Jenkins hadn't been
away and she hadn't been able to resist the opportunity
of spending an hour here on her own.

Something else had brought her here this afternoon,
she knew, apart from the chance of having a look around
without Quentin or Jenkins watching her, but she hadn't
faced this yet. For a while she sat on the gate into the
field where the horses grazed, talking idly to Hector and
the little mare, who came to see what she was doing.

Quentin hadn't told her not to go to the cottage where
she had lived, but he had forbidden her to go further
than the stables, which must be the same thing. With
Jenkins always around, keeping, she suspected, a wary
eye on her, she hadn't attempted to disobey, so Quentin
had probably decided she had forgotten, or wanted to
forget, all about the little house in the woods.

Which wasn't so. Gina was sometimes consumed by a
great urge to revisit the cottage. For one thing, she often
wondered what had happened to her father's books. Nor
could she get rid of some faint feelings of guilt and remorse. John might not have been the best of fathers, but
it seemed that she had abandoned his memory without so
much as a backward glance. It was difficult to remember
his acts of kindness, for they had been few, yet when he
had been in one of his good moods he had often sat and
talked to her, and his conversation had always been interesting and informative. She recognised now that he
had been an extremely intelligent man whose life had tra-
gically taken the wrong turning, and she was beset by the
conviction that she might, if she had tried harder, have

helped him more than she had done. Many a time, as she
had asked questions and listened to Charles talking to her
about her mother, she had wished things might have been
different, that her parents could still have been alive and
together.

But for all her conscience troubled her, Quentin's influence was strong. She felt more like a criminal than a duti-
ful daughter as she slid from the gate and made her way
towards the woods.

The path leading to the cottage had never been easy,
but she soon discovered that in places it was now almost
overgrown. Quentin must have forgotten his resolve to
clean up the woods, for she could see no sign of anything
having been done. They were much the same as they had
always been. So much for his hurry to evict them from
the cottage, she thought bitterly, pushing her way with
difficulty towards it.

She was surprised to find, on reaching it, that it hadn't
changed. The door wasn't locked and even inside it was,
like the woods, much the same. It didn't smell musty and
she frowned, wondering if someone had been keeping it
aired. Perhaps Quentin meant to restore it, when he got
round to it, rather than knock it down.

Taking a quick breath, she opened the door of her
father's bedroom, to find it empty and his books gone.
The room had been completely stripped, unlike the rest
of the cottage, which appeared to have been left exactly
as it was. There was nothing at all in John's room to
remind her of anything. Gently she closed the door, curious as to why she didn't feel overwhelmed. Well, it was
no use pretending a great sorrow. John would be the last
to expect it. At times, his cynicism had been worse than
Quentin's.

In the kitchen she sat for a while, letting memories
crowd in on her. She didn't see the old-fashioned grate,
where even the driest of wood had often been reluctant to
burn, she only saw the past. It was strange how, looking

back, she could see her life must have been one long
struggle, yet, in some ways, she had found it more satisfy-
ing than her present mode of living. Sometime in the near
future, she must find something to do. A job might help
to give some new purpose to her life and help to dispel
such curiously restless feelings.

Then, quickly ashamed of herself, she brushed away a
tear of self-pity, reminding herself of all her grandfather
and Liza had done for her.

Around the cottage a light wind sprang up, rustling
through the summer leaves on the trees. Then came a
footstep behind her, on the stone floor, bringing her stum-
bling sharply to her feet. As she turned, her eyes widened
in astonishment. It was Quentin, and she couldn't remember seeing him so angry—not, at least, since she used
to live here.

CHAPTER SEVEN

'WHAT are you doing here?' Gina whispered, her face white as she rubbed another tear from her cheek. 'I thought you were in Paris?'

'That was cancelled because of illness. Some other chap's, not mine,' Quentin replied grimly. 'I was having lunch when I suddenly realised that with Jenkins gone you wouldn't be able to get here fast enough.'

She tried to bluff it out with an indifferent shrug. 'Does it matter all that much?'

'Naturally it matters,' he snapped.

Again she shrugged, and she saw it increased his fury. 'I could have been and gone.'

'No, I rang my mother. She said you hadn't been this morning, so I knew it would be later.' As he moved closer, his mouth tightened as he noted her vivid hair tumbling about her shoulders, tangled from its contact with the trees. 'Why did you come when I asked you to stay away from the cottage, Gina?'

'Why did you want me to stay away?' she countered.

His hand came out to touch her face impatiently. 'Aren't these tears sufficient explanation? You've been crying. Isn't that reason enough?'

'I wasn't crying . . .' she was about to say—over that, when he cut her off curtly.

'Don't lie to me, my child.'

Such an unfair accusation shattered her composure completely. 'I'm not lying,' she cried. 'If I seem to be doing things behind your back, it's because I could never hope to win any other way. Not with you!'

'Gina!' his voice rasped, 'would you mind telling me

exactly what I've done to deserve this?'

'You can't remember?' Hysteria bubbled in her throat, while her eyes widened on his icy ones in sparkling contempt. 'You treated me horribly when I lived here. You never did a thing to help John. Your father did pay me something for looking after the horses, but you never gave me a penny. Quite often I had nothing to eat, thanks to you.' She knew this wasn't strictly true, but it only seemed to goad her further. 'You were mean and domineering, often cruel, and if you've changed since there has to be a reason!'

His face went white, and she felt a fleeting sense of triumph that she had shocked him. 'Have you quite finished?' he asked coldly.

When she nodded numbly, he said, 'You could have told me you hadn't enough to eat.'

'You mean people in my circumstances shouldn't allow themselves the luxury of pride. You must have guessed?'

'I didn't.' His voice roughened. 'Yes, maybe I should have done, but it all happened so quickly.'

'One can always find an excuse.'

'I wasn't even looking for one.'

'Just honest explanations,' she jeered, her eyes filling with wild tears.

'Gina, stop it!'

'Why should I?' She blinked her tears away with a fierce defiance. 'You always avoided the truth where I was concerned. I was something you didn't like, under your feet. You humiliated and hurt me, made me work in your house.'

'Gina, for God's sake, will you please shut up!' His eyes blazed so she thought they would scorch her. 'You don't even begin to understand, and while you're in this mood I won't try and make you. It's possibly doing you good, getting this all off your chest, even if it's knocking hell out of me. But I'm wiser than you and you'd better face it.' Harshly he enlarged, as she opened her mouth as if to question it, 'This, for instance. I told you not to come here.'

'No, you didn't.'

'I told you not to go beyond the stables.'

'Because of your guilty conscience? You threw my father and me out of our home so you could have it demolished, and you haven't done a thing about it. We could have been here yet.'

'Will you shut up!' He was speaking now between his teeth, and while she sensed he was controlling his temper with difficulty, she was driven to continue taunting him.

'No, I won't!'

'This way I'll make you!'

'No!' Guessing his intentions too late, she couldn't escape when his arms came out and snatched her to him.

She had a frightening glimpse of his eyes, dark with leashed anger, and what might have been desire, before his hard lips hit hers, forcing her tightly closed ones apart. For all the cruel strength he used she felt an immediate response rushing through her. His mouth searched hers, probing every corner, until she melted helplessly against him, her clenched fists unfolding to curve tensely around his shoulders.

She moaned faintly and felt his muscles go taut under the thin clothes he wore, but he didn't let her go. He went on kissing her with unabated anger until her whole body was on fire and lax against his. Roughly his hand went to her blouse, pulling open the buttons, finding the softness underneath, holding her tightly when, with a gasp, she would have drawn away. She wanted to fight him, but instead found herself submitting weakly as his arms tightened fiercely.

It was minutes later before he lifted his head again, to ease her slightly away from the strong beat of his heart. 'Perhaps now you'll be willing to marry me?' he said grimly, narrowly surveying her warmly flushed cheeks.

His curt query shocking her into abrupt awareness, she

opened her eyes to stare at him in amazement. 'No!' she whispered. 'Never. You can't be serious?'

Ignoring her startled plea, his voice hardened and she was frightened by his expression as he stared down at her. 'If you don't agree, I'll have you now. God knows I've wanted you long enough. I realise, though, that the exact change in our relationship hasn't been easy, but I've tried to help, not hurt you.'

'You must be joking!' she gasped, intending, in spite of owning the truth of his words, to defy him for ever.

His eyes glittered. 'I don't have to put up with insults from a skinny little redhead any longer,' he retorted savagely. 'I want you and intend having you. It's up to you which way.'

'You wouldn't dare touch me!' Knowing her first flicker of fear, she caught her breath.

'Wouldn't I?' His mirthless laughter was utterly quelling. 'After this afternoon, I assure you, you could be only too ready to agree to anything.'

Frantically she tried to hit out at him, as the grim determination on his face convinced her he meant everything he said, but he simply caught her arm, jamming it down by her side. As she gasped with pain, he muttered something under his breath and swung her high in his arms. As if she were a feather, and without hesitation, he carried her through to her old bedroom. When, wishing feverishly she hadn't aroused his anger, Gina tried to speak, she was unable to utter a single word.

She had no chance to speak again, for the last breath seemed knocked out of her as Quentin threw her on the bed and slid down beside her. When she turned her head from him desperately, he merely caught her chin, turning her back. Then his mouth renewed its contact with her own with passionate intensity. She wanted to resist, but the pressure of his lips aroused such powerful emotions that she lost all inclination. Without being aware of it, she found herself relaxing, clinging to him, offering herself to his demanding mouth and exploring hands as though she had no desire left but to please him.

He shrugged out of his shirt, then removed hers, his hands and then his mouth caressing her throbbing breasts. He had her twisting frantically away from him, moaning with pain from the roughness of his chin, before pleasure took over and she twisted back, her arms going around his neck to hold him even closer.

Sensuously, as she stirred, his gaze slid slowly over the slender whiteness of her limbs, then he groaned out her name, his voice husky with emotion as he pushed her back against the mattress with the hard force of his body. The next instant she was gasping with shock as he came completely over her, his intentions very clear, even to one of her complete innocence.

'Quentin!' she was struggling through the avalanche of passion and desire to find enough strength to wrench her too vulnerable mouth from under his. 'Quentin,' she gasped, 'I give in . . .!'

Again he groaned, becoming utterly still, so she wasn't sure he had heard her. Or if he had replied and she hadn't heard him, for the blood was drumming so loudly in her ears she could hear nothing else.

At last he spoke, as if it were an effort. 'What do you mean by that, exactly?'

'Oh,' her already hot cheeks grew hotter, as she understood how her own reply might have been interpreted, 'I—I mean I'll marry you.'

When he still didn't move she wondered if she had left it too late. But suddenly it didn't seem to matter any more. She could hear the harshness of his breathing, feel the heaviness of his hard, muscular body. It drove every other consideration from her head. Blindly she began searching for his mouth again, pressing her hands flat against his chest, feeling the roughness of it tantalising her soft fingers. 'Please, Quentin,' she whispered, 'love me, love me.'

Abruptly he let her go, rising swiftly to his feet. Instinctively she knew he had found it almost impossible, yet when she blindly put out an arm to stop him, he shook her off roughly. 'No more,' he snapped, thrusting into his shirt and tucking it into his trousers. As he finished his task, he walked over to the window, presumably giving her a few moments to do the same.

'So—when's the wedding going to be?' he asked, turning back to her at last and staring at her quite impersonally, although there was a white grimness to his mouth. 'This week, next week? No longer.'

'I thought you were asking me?' she faltered, thinking this must be the strangest proposal a girl had ever had. In a bare room, in a condemned cottage, without a word of love exchanged. Why did Quentin want to marry her? To make amends for the past, or because he was attracted to her? Or because a wife might be useful? Somewhere among these three possibilities might lie the answer?

'I'll leave the final decision to you,' he replied magnanimously, 'but within those limits.'

Angrily she said, 'It's not long enough. What would my grandfather think, for one thing?'

'I don't much care, but somehow I don't think he'll object, Gina.' He came to sit by her again on the narrow bed. 'He knows I'm not a patient man.'

'Don't you care for me at all?' she burst out.

'Yes, I care,' he said soberly, his eyes intent on her face. 'Ours has been a difficult relationship, but I've wanted you since the night I rescued you from the lake. I've considered you mine from that moment, but you're older now, which makes a difference.'

'Does it?' she asked hollowly, wondering if she could believe him.

'Damn it all, Gina, haven't I said enough? Might I ask how you feel about me?'

She flinched from his weighted sarcasm. He enquired

as if he were interviewing her for a job! and while she
knew how he could make her feel, she had no clear idea
of her feelings otherwise. Once she had thought she loved
him, but he had killed that emotion long ago. Hadn't he?

Unhappily, she avoided a straight answer. 'Getting
married is your idea, not mine.'

With his eyes fixed on her, he might have been following the drift of her thoughts exactly. 'If the idea was in
my head, Gina, maybe you helped put it there. You respond very passionately.'

There was a world of experience in the glance he ran
over her and she felt a flush of embarrassment rise to her
face. 'I hope you aren't marrying me just for that!' she
retorted tartly. 'Anyway, you could be mistaken.'

'I don't think so,' he drawled. 'But let's not worry too
much, too soon. The future will take care of itself.' Bending his head, he kissed her again, as if to still further
indignation, and much as she tried to resist her mouth
clung to his with a gasp of undisguised pleasure. Slowly
he eased the pressure he exerted, teasing her mouth open
with a gentle thumb before placing moist, warm lips over
hers again.

Fire spread within her, along her nerves, entering her
bloodstream, dispensing to centre points of sensation.
Blindly she clutched his hand, placing it wantingly over
her heart, wanting his touch, his caresses almost greedily.

'Do you still need convincing?' he mocked derisively,
although as he drew back she saw he was pale.

'Didn't you ever try to persuade Blanche like that?' She
didn't know why she asked, but she had to find some
release from the tension inside her.

'Leave Blanche out of this!' He was suddenly so curt,
Gina was startled. 'You're the only girl who's any use to
me now.'

'Wasn't it always my role?' she returned, with match-
ing shortness, 'to be useful? Ever since I can remember.'

Suddenly unable to bear staying there any longer, she jumped to her feet and almost ran from the room, her sentence trailing off behind her.

More slowly Quentin followed and, as they left the cottage, rather than continue about Blanche she attacked him another way. 'What did you do with my father's books?'

'What do you think?' he closed the door firmly—and locked it. 'I kept them for you.'

Glancing at him with sudden hatred, she noticed he pocketed the key. 'You burnt them, of course.'

'Always so ready to believe the worst, aren't you, Gina? What a delightful wife you're going to make!'

'No doubt you think you'll soon have me licked into shape? What a good start for you, that you know all my faults. When you've had time to consider them, you mightn't think marriage such a good idea, after all.'

He smiled sardonically at her flushed face. 'Don't worry—it's going to happen.'

From past experience Gina knew she could only defy Quentin so far, and never yet had she succeeded in winning a battle against him. If she hoped to win this one, instinct warned her she would have to be devious. She wanted revenge for the past, not his caresses, she argued, but these she might have to endure before she could reap her revenge and be rid of him for good.

'I'd rather you didn't say anything to my grandfather for a day or two,' she said slowly as they emerged from the woods.

'Why not?' Grimly Quentin dusted some twigs from his broad shoulders.

'You were going to have the woods cleared?'

'Gina! Please answer my question.'

She shrugged. 'He seemed worried at lunch. It's probably not much, but he has seemed rather down lately.'

'Our engagement might cheer him up. Look at it that way.'

'I'm frightened there really is something and it only adds to his worries,' she faltered, trying to decide honestly if this was the real reason she wanted to keep her relationship with Quentin secret.

Quentin glanced at her thoughtfully. 'Stop worrying, Gina. Leave your grandfather to me. There won't be any problems.' He took hold of her arm as she bent her head evasively, 'Come on, cheer up. How about seeing if Mrs Worth can spare a cup of tea? You look as if you could do with one.'

Mrs Worth not only made them a cup of tea, she produced fresh scones, white and fluffy, fat with strawberry jam and cream. They sat down at the kitchen table and Gina was surprised to find how hungry she was.

'Something's given you an appetite?' Quentin teased.

She flushed, aware that Mrs Worth was trying to hide her curiosity. As Quentin laid his hand over hers and began playing idly with her fingers, Mrs Worth almost dropped the teapot and even Myra's eyes widened.

'Do you think, Mrs Worth,' Quentin tightened his hold on Gina's suddenly tense fingers, 'you could manage a small dinner party for tomorrow night? Just Sir Charles and Mrs Cunningham and of course my—er—that is, Gina. It's going to be rather special.'

Gina couldn't resist the small kick she aimed at his ankle under the table, but he didn't so much as flinch. The only change in him was the deepening satisfaction in his eyes as they rested on her rosy cheeks. If he had stood up and made an announcement, there and then, he couldn't have made it any clearer. Gina could see this from the smug understanding on Mrs Worth's face and the dawning excitement on Myra's.

When Mrs Worth agreed, quite breathlessly for her, Quentin said he would speak to his mother. 'You can arrange the details with her later,' he smiled, leaving the kitchen with Gina.

'What had you to do that for?' she asked angrily, as he

put her into her car. 'I asked you to wait, but you may as well have put it in the evening press!'

He grinned, with infuriating indifference. 'I can trust Mrs Worth's discretion. She probably has guessed, but I didn't actually say anything.'

Gina's green eyes blazed. 'You haven't told your mother yet, nor my grandfather. How do you know they'll be free tomorrow night, even if they like what you have to tell them?'

'I intend to arrange it,' he said smoothly. 'I have to return to London shortly, but I'll see my mother before I go, and your grandfather in the morning. You can take it there'll be no objections,' he added sardonically, gently closing her car door.

The arrogance of the man! Gina clenched her teeth on a frustrated sigh as she drove away. Why did he insist he wanted to marry her when so often he didn't appear to even like her? If he hadn't been so well off she might have suspected him of marrying her for her grandfather's money, but it couldn't be that!

She was back at Bourne Court before she realised there was nothing to stop her changing her mind about marrying him. He couldn't really force her to, no matter what he said, and she could always appeal to her grandfather, if Quentin tried to use pressure. Yet, facing a moment of truth, she became conscious that she wanted this marriage with Quentin. She wasn't sure why, and shrank from delving too deeply, but somehow the thought of belonging to him didn't seem so shattering any more, although she suspected their actual marriage might be!

Deliberately she kept out of sight next morning when Quentin called. From her bedroom window she watched him drive up to the front door and from the top of the stairs she had heard him being shown into her grandfather's study. Her heart thudding uneasily, she returned to her room, trying to imagine the conversation that must be taking place.

Dismally she glanced at her tired face, the dark circles under her eyes, which would have betrayed to someone much less observant than Quentin that she had slept little during the night. The scene in the cottage bedroom had kept returning to mock her. Time and time again, she felt herself go hot with shame as she remembered the depth of her own response and Quentin's frank reference to it. It wasn't until dawn broke that she had managed to convince herself she wasn't really like that and it wouldn't happen again.

Tautly she had decided she must take good care not to be alone with Quentin until they were married, and then she would think twice before granting him any marital rights. She wasn't so innocent that she didn't know he might expect them, but as they weren't in love it might not take much to keep him at arm's length. Sensing his pride, she didn't think for a moment he would be prepared to fight for his rights if she didn't give in to him willingly. If he did, she would tell him quite frankly he must look elsewhere.

Determined to avoid him this morning, she slipped out and walked several miles over the downs, heedless that her feet were soon soaked in the dewy grass. Her thoughts were still muddled when she returned to the house, but Quentin had gone. Only Charles and Liza were there.

Liza rose and hugged her, so did Charles.

Liza said coyly, 'Quentin's been here, darling, asking for your hand. You knew he was coming?'

Charles sighed. 'If only your dear mother had chosen so wisely!' He cleared his throat. 'I take it you're happy, child?'

There seemed nothing else to do but nod and say yes and hug them both back.

Liza beamed, 'Quentin's older than you, but he's very clever, you know. A lot of women are going to envy you.'

Again Gina nodded, without much expression. She saw

her grandfather didn't appear quite as jubilant as Liza, but decided this might be because he didn't want to lose her.

That evening at Briarly, she tried to insist on three months before marriage, but Quentin ground it down to less than three weeks.

'Will you live here or in London?' her grandfather asked him rather anxiously.

'Here, most of the time,' Quentin replied, without consulting Gina.

Mrs Hurst sighed. 'I shall have to think of looking for a small place of my own. Briarly is Quentin's now, of course.'

A knot of indignation at the high-handed way Quentin was overruling everyone made Gina exclaim quickly, 'Please don't let me drive you away, Mrs Hurst. Briarly's surely big enough for three, and as Quentin will be in town most days we can keep each other company.'

'Leave it to me, Gina,' Quentin's voice was suddenly cold. 'There'll be plenty of time to sort everything out, once we're back from our honeymoon.'

Gina glanced at him quickly as her heart leaped. Need he look so far ahead? He was so tall, dark and elegant it was very easy to forget how ruthless he could be. 'Will you have time for a honeymoon?' she asked. 'You're always so busy.'

'I intend having one,' he returned her flickering glance coolly. 'You might think it's going to be a bit of an anticlimax when you've just been for a trip around the world, but I assure you this will be quite different.'

Charles coughed, while Mrs Hurst looked slightly embarrassed and Liza pretended to. Gina, feeling her own cheeks go hot, kept her eyes on the table, refusing to admit another lurch in her stomach. She wondered how Quentin's mother really felt about their engagement. She hadn't said anything, but Gina had gained the impression that she was slightly stunned.

Quentin had sent the announcement to the news-papers, so by the next morning everyone knew. He had asked her to accompany him to London, and Gina felt guilty about leaving Liza to cope with the telephone calls already coming in. Not that she felt able to speak to people herself. Looking back, it seemed she hadn't been allowed time to draw breath since that afternoon in the cottage. Quentin had taken over, arranging everything so quickly and irrevocably that she was only just beginning to realise how committed she was. As he drove her to London, she was so edgy about it all she couldn't relax. She felt nervous, disturbed by his nearness yet unwilling to admit it.

They didn't talk much. She concluded there would be little he would want to actually discuss with her. He would have everything cut and dried. As always her opinion would count for little, and the habits of a lifetime weren't easy to dispose of.

The city streets were as crowded as usual, which made conversation impossible. It wasn't until they reached his place of business that Gina had an opportunity to ask what his plans were. She knew a ring was high up on his agenda, but this wouldn't take all day.

Believing he would suggest she should keep herself amused until lunchtime, at least, he surprised her by saying, 'Come up with me, Gina. I shan't be long.'

'I could meet you somewhere, later.' She held back.

'Must you be awkward?' Glancing impatiently at his watch, Quentin took her arm, seeming to imply, by the tight set of his lips, that she always had been. 'I don't want you running around London on your own.'

'I wouldn't get lost!'

'Wouldn't you?' With withering emphasis he stared at her.

As the lift whispered upwards, she decided it was use-less to protest any further, and, as she had never been here before, she could always satisfy her curiosity.

There appeared to be enough floors, and enough staff to run the QE11. Quentin's own office seemed the height of luxury. His secretary was there, and her unflattering astonishment was unconcealed for a fleeting moment when Quentin introduced Gina as his fiancée. Obviously she considered Gina too young, or too unsuitable. Gina occupied herself, while waiting for Quentin, trying to decide which it was.

An hour later he appeared and asked Miss Bell, who was still shooting Gina acid-sweet glances, to bring coffee. Gina felt in need of it, but while she drank two cups Quentin scarcely touched his. Sensing a certain tension in him, she suggested he have something stronger, but he replied cynically that he usually managed to do without until later in the day.

He took her to a jewellers with such superb decor she scarcely dared breathe, and the ring he eventually slipped on her finger almost stopped her breath altogether. She didn't see the price, but she was sure it was so costly she would be terrified of losing it.

He kissed her, while the obliging assistant looked the other way, and she managed to keep her lips cool and steady. But in the taxi that bore them towards the hotel he had chosen for lunch, he pulled her to him savagely. This time he didn't stop until she slumped against him, her lips soft with the warmth of surrender, her heart racing under his hand.

'That's better,' he said, as if she were a backward child. 'When I kiss you in future I don't want to be reminded of an iceberg.'

The fiery sensation of his kiss did nothing to calm her taut nerves. If anything it made her aware that she was taking on more than she could manage.

'What sort of women have you been used to?' she blazed at him softly, and was pleased to note that her shaft had gone home. His face went grim and he didn't look at her with pleasure any more.

Nevertheless, over lunch he was charming, making Gina wonder cynically if he had decided an openly antagonistic bride wouldn't do his public image much good. After lunch he took her to see his London home.

'It might be the last chance before the wedding,' he said, as he showed her over the superb flat near Regent's Park.

He employed a man who did the cooking and cleaning, but he wasn't there. 'He takes a day off occasionally when I don't need him,' Quentin explained. 'But when I do he's quite willing to work a seven-day week.'

Gina liked the flat, but she liked Briarly better. Secretly she hoped Quentin wouldn't expect her to stay in London very much. She rather wished his man had been here as being alone with him was making her uneasy. She was reminded of how he had been at the cottage, and of her own reactions.

'This will be our bedroom when we stay in Town,' Quentin opened the door of a room of generous proportions containing a huge double bed. The glitter in his grey eyes mocked her as he saw her startled surprise. 'I think it's an improvement on the one at the cottage, don't you, but if you don't like the decor you can always change it.'

'It looks very nice,' she mumbled hastily, retreating from the bed with a strange sense of irrational excitement. She couldn't see herself spending the night in that, entwined in Quentin's arms. He could be too demanding a lover, forcing her to give in to him, and a bed like that could only aid him in achieving his desires. 'Twin beds would be nicer,' she said faintly, 'and more in fashion.'

'That's one thing I won't have,' he replied so adamantly that fire streaked along her veins. 'You sleep with me, and to hell with fashion!'

'I—I didn't ask for separate rooms!' she hedged.

'Well, separate beds are out,' he assured her. 'I don't believe in them either.'

'You have to consider me.'

'I'm quite aware of that.' His voice was taunting, twisting his words. 'It might be a good idea if you began taking a look at yourself. You might discover you want me almost as much as I want you.'

'Don't be so silly,' she retorted hastily, her face burning. 'Of course I don't!'

With a grim smile he came closer, pulling her to him as he had done in the taxi, only this time he wasn't so cruel. One eyebrow lifted with mock humour. 'You need convincing?'

'No, I do not.' Wriggling in his embrace, she entreated pleadingly when he didn't let her go. 'Please, Quentin—we can decide about the bed later. It isn't important.'

'Some things are.'

'Such as getting your own way?'

'Apart from the bed—over what?'

Feeling oddly short of breath, she gulped some more down, wishing his hard body wasn't so near her own. 'Over getting married so soon.'

'Three weeks is my limit.' His eyes flicking comprehensively over her left her in no doubt about his meaning. 'You can please yourself.'

'You've more than enough will power when you choose to exercise it,' she said fiercely.

'Not where you're concerned,' his voice went husky as his eyes reached her mouth. 'With you I can't.'

'Can't or won't?'

'Either way it's getting impossible.' His arms tightened as he bent his head. 'Must you go on talking?'

The day was hot. Gina wore only a light suit and had discarded the top. It hung downstairs with Quentin's jacket. Now, as he caught her to him, she could feel the hardness of his muscles crushing her breasts through the thinness of silky material.

'Kiss me,' he muttered thickly.

'Quentin!' she protested, her heart pounding against

his chest. 'Aren't you forgetting we're going to be married? We'll have plenty of time for this sort of thing then.'

'Damn it all, Gina,' he groaned, 'will you stop making stupid remarks!'

She was only trying to protect herself! With Quentin her emotions so easily got out of hand. While certain she disliked him, she was finding it ever more difficult to resist him. Now, as he held her, her heart raced and her limbs felt weak. She was ready to admit that most of her remarks over the last five minutes had been stupid, but this had only been to hide what lay underneath. Could she pray that if she obliged with a brief kiss he would leave it at that? Obediently she lifted her taut face, making no further effort to avoid his impatient mouth.

As his mouth met hers he closed the door, isolating them in the warm silence of the room. She could feel her heart racing out of control as the pressure of his mouth deepened and his hands began touching her intimately. He pushed up her thin vest top, then her bra, his hands finding her shapely breasts, stroking them gently.

Gina felt herself responding to his caresses with a helpless moan, whereas she had been so determined to resist him. Passion flared between them, making Quentin's mouth suddenly urgent on her parted lips. With a groan almost as helpless as her own, he ran his hands down her spine to the very end of it, moving deliberately against her with the thrust of his hard male body. When she gasped and cried out it did nothing to cool his obvious desire.

His hands came back to her face, shaping it as he covered it with deep, drugging kisses. He kissed her until she began returning his kisses wildly and ecstasy flooded through them both. Then he was lifting her, holding her tightly to him, kissing her deeply, sensually, as he walked with her towards the bed.

Passion moved so overwhelmingly in Gina that she

didn't protest any more. She was potently aware they couldn't get near enough each other and everything else faded. Pushing trembling arms around his neck, she murmured his name breathlessly, her voice shaking.

CHAPTER EIGHT

IT was as if the sound of his name, gasped out in such a fashion, made Quentin realise what was happening. Before they reached the bed he dropped her to her feet, and she heard breath being dragged into his empty lungs as he steadied her.

'No, Gina!' His face was pale, his hands unsteady. She could never recall seeing him like this before.

She was trembling so much herself, she protested, without realising fully what she was saying. 'You said you wanted me?'

'And I believe you want me, which makes it mutual,' his voice was harshly derisive, 'but I don't really want you this way.'

'At the cottage——' she began tearfully.

Curtly, he cut in, his eyes dark, 'Yes—at the cottage—where you went of your own accord, and I sought you because I was concerned for your welfare, things almost got out of hand. But that was something that just happened. It wasn't planned. If I made love to you now, you could say I'd brought you here deliberately, which I did, but not with seduction in mind.'

'Didn't you suspect it might happen?' She knew it must seem as if she were goading him, but somehow she couldn't stop herself.

'No!' he exclaimed. Then his face hardened with an imperceptible irritation. 'Damn it, Gina, I thought I was capable of handling anything like that. I admit the possibility did cross my mind, but I've been in tricky situations before and never lost control. With you it seems to be different. I don't seem sure any more.'

'I can't remember you being unsure about anything,' she retorted unevenly, having been subject to his cool authority all her life. 'Your father would have called it common sense.'

He ignored her dryness. 'Common sense wouldn't have influenced either of us if we'd got as far as that bed—and you know it! You're not that innocent. In fact I'm beginning to wonder what innocence is.' His eyes smouldered over her, lingering cynically on her hot cheeks. 'You respond so wholeheartedly you would put many an experienced woman to shame.'

'Well, you've known a lot!'

'No, I haven't. Not intimately,' he returned coolly. 'Affairs take time, and I've never had a lot of that to spare.'

'Is it their gain and your loss or the other way round?' she queried smoothly, trying to punish him for his remarks.

Instead of rising to the bait, he took a determined hold of her arm. 'Let's get out of here, Gina,' he said, steering her through the door. 'Words can be as challenging and as intoxicating as actions sometimes, and I'm not sure I can take any more.'

On the way home she couldn't sit still and relax. She felt curiously keyed up, just beginning to be conscious of the strain of unsatisfied feelings. After London the countryside sped by. Quentin drove fast and was as silent as he had been as they had driven in that morning, but this evening his silence wasn't as welcome.

It caused an uneasiness, making her touch abruptly on a subject she had meant to avoid. 'Grandfather is going to miss me. He says he's had me for so short a time. After we're married I'll have to see him every day.'

'I expect he'll survive,' Quentin replied idly. 'He still has his house and grounds to keep him occupied.'

'And he has Liza.'

'She's a tower of strength.'

'I still think we should wait longer, Quentin.'

'No,' she noticed his well kept hands tighten on the steering wheel, 'I won't wait, Gina,' his voice dropped so she had to strain to hear. 'I can't.'

Frowning, she stared at the green, rolling downs. Why couldn't he? For a moment he seemed quite desperate. If she could believe he ever could be. Yet it was difficult to interpret the note in his voice as anything else. Feeling a warmth of trembling anticipation, she kept her eyes on the road. She wanted him to want her so she could have the triumph of rejecting him, but she wasn't sure she could fight him indefinitely. If his feelings were beginning to be involved she mightn't find it possible to keep him at a distance for ever—but would she want to? Perhaps, after he had suffered a little, she might have to forgive him . . .?

It had been a long day and Gina was relieved when Quentin made no arrangements to see her later, as he dropped her off at Bourne Court. After helping her from the car he refused her offer of a drink. 'Thanks,' he said curtly, 'but I have work to catch up on. Tell your grandfather I'll give him a ring after dinner. He'll know what about.'

'What about?' a smile of curiosity lit her face briefly. 'Can't I know? You sound very mysterious.'

'No,' but he didn't deny it as he dropped a light, almost indifferent kiss on her mouth. 'Curiosity is sometimes better left unsatisfied. Run along, there's a good girl.'

Sometimes, Gina thought next morning, as she went out riding, Quentin treated her like a schoolgirl, which made it difficult to account for the occasions when, with his arms around her, he seemed to consider her very much a woman.

She felt the warmth of the sun on her head and raised her face to it, letting it caress her features softly. She had been almost relieved to get away from the house this morning. There had been something in the atmosphere she couldn't understand. Liza had talked of Gina's trousseau, insisting they ought to have a few days in London to gather it together. Gina had protested, perhaps more sharply than she ought to have done, that she had more than enough clothes left over from her world tour, many never yet worn. All she could possibly need was a wedding dress, which she could surely get without going to London.

Liza's face had immediately registered disapproval and Gina had been surprised when, having expected her grandfather to look the same way, he had unexpectedly declared himself in agreement with Gina. That there was no sense in buying new clothes, just for the sake of buying them.

Liza had looked ready to burst into tears of disappointment, and, because she had felt sorry for her, Gina had agreed to accompany her, that very afternoon, to what Liza maintained was a wonderful little dress shop. The only decent one outside London! Gina sighed as she envisaged the struggle which would undoubtedly ensue over the choice of her wedding dress.

So immersed was she in such troublesome thoughts, she didn't see Blanche Edgar until it was much too late to avoid her.

Blanche was riding a small black horse and she looked remarkably well on it. Gina would like to have told her so, but the awkwardness of the moment became apparent too quickly. Blanche had only known her as the girl who looked after Quentin's horses, then as his mother's maid—while she had had every expectation of marrying him herself. Gina couldn't help feeling sorry for her. For Blanche it must be dreadful to find Gina suddenly an heiress, and engaged to the man she had hoped to marry. But although Gina felt sorry for Blanche she couldn't help feeling sorry for herself, too, for in truth, Quentin loved neither of them. She couldn't, of course, very well say so.

As Gina groped uncertainly, and with not a little embarrassment for words, Blanche flicked her a far from flattering glance.

Without even pausing to say a polite good morning, she said coldly, 'It seems you've done very well for yourself, Gina.'

Gina controlled her temper with difficulty. Blanche did have some excuse for being insulting, but she didn't have to stay and listen. With a small nod she made to ride on.

She hadn't supposed Blanche would bother to try and stop her, and was startled by the sharp note in the other girl's voice as she did so. 'Wait a minute! I want to speak to you, to congratulate you on your engagement.'

Old habits die hard. Gina found herself obeying without intending to, for it was quite clear Blanche didn't wish her well in anything. Her silence appeared to annoy Blanche even more.

'Don't you think I'm being generous?' she snapped. 'Especially when Quentin was going to marry me.'

Sharply Gina bit her lip, while a curious sense of dread made her heart pound. At last she said, 'If you thought so, then I'm sorry.'

'I did more than think so!' Blanche's face flushed with hatred, she was obviously finding it an effort to remain calm. 'The breaking off of our relationship was, of course, mutual. I lost everything I'd been led to believe I would inherit and Quentin couldn't afford a poor wife.'

Gina's frown was faintly incredulous. 'I'm sure he doesn't need a rich one.'

'Doesn't he?' Blanche's voice was vindictive. 'Didn't you know, you little fool, he's lost a great deal of money? It's common knowledge. It's also well known that your grandfather is helping him. They've been together almost continually this last week. You might not have liked having no money, Gina, but how do you like being married for it?'

Shock froze Gina so still she couldn't speak as Blanche

pulled cruelly on her reins and whirled away from her. Horrified by what she had heard, Gina stared after her, until the little black horse was just a speck in the distance.

Could what Blanche told her be true? Had Quentin asked her to marry him so that Charles would be forced to help him out of financial difficulties? Dazed, she thought of Quentin's hurried proposal, the abrupt way he had made it. She had been so bemused by his lovemaking she hadn't noticed at the time, although she recalled now that she had wondered. She did remember he hadn't spoken like a man in love.

It should have occurred to her, but it was the one thing which hadn't. It had to be financial trouble which had driven him to reject Blanche and seek someone else. Neither Blanche or her brother would be able to help him. Bitterly Gina recalled him saying she was the only girl any use to him now. How true! Now that she realised what he was talking about, how very true—and trite— that statement was. And wasn't Blanche right? What a fool she had been to have swallowed it all unsuspectingly!

The dreadful thing was she couldn't bring herself to go to her grandfather and tell him the truth—that Quentin was simply marrying her to save his own skin. How was it, she wondered, in cold despair, that the old loyalties were still there? Had he guessed she could never betray him? He must have speculated wildly and should be made to pay for his folly, as other men did, instead of sitting quietly laughing!

It made her blindly angry that she didn't have the courage to be the one to expose him, for how could she bear to see Briarly sold—for it might come to that—and never to see Quentin again? Whatever he had done, wasn't he part of her? To lose him would be like losing a part of herself. It was suddenly too intolerable to even contemplate. Yet she couldn't sit here, wallowing in pity for him. She must refuse to allow such feelings to take over.

She had been unhappy about their marriage, unsure of

how Quentin felt about her, now she knew she had been right to distrust him. She might be trapped by her own feelings, but she would never give in to him, she would make his life hell! She would marry him, but tell him what she had learnt on their wedding night. He had a lot to answer for, both past and present! Her heart hardening with bitterness, Gina rode slowly home.

Charles Hearn came walking around the corner of the house as she drew up before it and immediately noticed her distraught face. 'Is anything wrong?' he asked with a frown as he opened the car door for her.

'Of course not.' She forced a brief smile, annoyed that she hadn't seen her grandfather approaching. 'Perhaps I've ridden too far.'

'Gina,' his frown hadn't disappeared, 'you are happy about marrying Quentin? You do love him?'

'Don't worry,' she smiled weakly, but let the moment when she might have confided in him pass, 'I've always loved Quentin.'

'It's worth any sacrifice to hear you say that,' Charles replied, his relief very evident.

As they went inside Gina realised this must be because Quentin had borrowed a large sum of money from him, but that he didn't mind if it was for her happiness.

It made her sense of bitterness increase when between then and their wedding, Quentin was kinder to her than he had ever been. They weren't alone much, and she suspected he deliberately avoided seeing a lot of her. Kindness was one thing, having to pretend a deeper affection quite another. He was busy, and she noted with scorn that he had several private sessions with her grandfather.

Neither man made any comment about the time they spent together and she didn't ask, but one evening, just before the wedding, Charles said something that enraged her. He told her he was selling the lease on his London house.

'It seems foolish to have two houses, now I'm getting older and you're getting married,' he explained.

'But what about Liza? She loves London.'

'Oh, she agrees with me,' Charles said uncomfortably.

Unconvinced, Gina stared at him doubtfully. 'I suppose she can always stay with Quentin and me, whenever she wants to?'

'I believe that's what she's hoping you might say, but she won't be visiting you very often. Since you came she seems to like being here.'

'I'm leaving . . .' Gina said helplessly.

'But you'll still be near.'

'Yes, of course I will be.' She gave him a brilliant smile while her heart was breaking. She knew how much he loved his London home. He had so many friends there and was still young enough to enjoy a few weeks in London, as a change. He must have let his house go to help Quentin.

The day of the wedding arrived and the ceremony and reception were soon over.

'Everything's gone off remarkably well,' Quentin's mother observed, with a kind of surprised satisfaction as they left on their honeymoon, and she said goodbye.

Dutifully, Gina kissed her. Mrs Hurst had been so pleasant to her lately that she wondered if she knew about the money Quentin had received from Charles. Ruefully, Gina was aware how it was beginning to poison her relationship with both Quentin and his mother. But perhaps she was being unfair. Perhaps Mrs Hurst knew nothing about it.

They flew to Vienna. Quentin, she realised, had been disappointed over her choice, but he had left it to her. He hadn't quarrelled with her decision, even though he didn't pretend to understand it. He would have preferred the West Indies or America—he had even suggested Australia. He had named places, remote and beautiful, places for lovers. Watching her closely, he had been obviously puzzled by her fleeting expression of digust as she had wondered angrily how he dared be so extravagant with someone else's money. Bleakly she had shaken her head and settled for Vienna.

Had he been relieved? She thought so. Possibly he was thinking of Blanche and her older sophistication. Gina knew she had a long way to go before she reached Blanche's standard, but Quentin should have thought of that before he married another girl. Vienna would do as well as anywhere else for a couple of days, which was all their honeymoon would probably amount to after she told him what she knew. She had planned this as the grand finale to an evening spent dining and dancing and letting him expect she was ready to be a loving and obedient wife. She might be one day, but not for a long time. Not until Quentin paid back every penny he had taken from her grandfather. Only then might she reconsider.

Almost aching with disillusionment, she asked Quentin if he would get her a drink of fruit squash. Every time she thought of the coming evening her mouth went dry. They were travelling first class and there was a free serve-yourself bar, and she watched with dull eyes as he walked obligingly towards it.

In Austria, at the Schwechat Airport, some twenty minutes from Vienna, he quickly dispensed with formalities. Gina had got used to flying with Charles and Liza, and certainly they were experienced travellers, but Quentin seemed to achieve twice as much in half the time. It did occur to her this might be partly due to the fact that the eyes of the female staff, both on and off the plane, were frequently trained on his dark good looks. He never had to endure long waits before attracting attention. It wasn't merely his looks, she conceded, it was his remarkable virility. She wondered how these same girls would feel if they knew he was capable of fraud and deceit.

When Quentin had agreed eventually to Vienna, he

had taken over all the arrangements. The hotel they were taken to was the last word in luxury, but rather than impress it only added to Gina's sense of grievance. After they were shown into a beautiful suite she found it very hard to hide her resentment.

As Quentin, with another thoughtful glance at her, idly unlocked her suitcase and opened it for her, she snatched up a silky dress, without glancing to see if it was anything special, and locked herself in the bathroom. After showering quickly, she dried and slipped it over her head. It was after nine and in spite of the turmoil inside her Gina felt hungry. Neither Quentin nor she had eaten much on the plane as they hadn't been hungry, and Quentin had suggested it might be better to wait until they got here.

He had changed, too, when she came out, and was so superbly handsome her heart skipped a beat. He came towards her, his eyes amused yet guarded, dropping a light kiss on her full mouth. 'You don't have to lock the bathroom door now,' he grinned. 'I'm your husband, in case you've forgotten that impressive ceremony we went through.'

She lowered her lashes so he wouldn't see the sudden longing in her eyes. If only things had been different, she wouldn't have wanted to go down for dinner. The only hunger she felt would have been for him.

'Gina?' His voice deepened as his hands went to her shoulders, as if he felt the same way.

Quickly she pulled from his tightening grip, yet not so quickly as to give the impression she was rejecting him. 'I'm ravenous!' She curved her pink, inviting lips in a deliberate smile.

'Let's go down then, by all means,' he replied patiently, his strong features immediately controlled as he took her arm possessively and steered her from the room.

'You're looking beautiful tonight.' Staring at her over the table in the restaurant, he took in the silky fall of her glowing hair, her young silky skin and bare shoulders. 'Exactly as a girl should look on her honeymoon.'

Again she smiled at him, remembering it was part of her plan to encourage him. Inside she echoed with the hollowness of derision. Whoever heard of a bride having to force herself to smile at her new husband?

'Shall we dance?' he suggested, with an eagerness which made her quiver as she rose to her feet. The food they were eating was delicious, but she left it without a second thought.

In Quentin's arms the attraction he had for her increased. Her heart pounded as he made little attempt to disguise his desire. Dear Quentin—who had bullied and dominated her for most of her short life, whom she had hated and loved ever since she could remember. How easy it would be to give in, to let him take over completely, to forget what he was. He pulled her close to him and she could feel the deliberately arousing movements of his strong thighs locked with hers. But only for a short time dared she allow him to think she had surrendered. Because they were on the dance floor she let him mould her ever closer, his lips to rest on her cheek as she lay helplessly against his shoulder. Inexorably his arms tightened until they might almost have been as one.

After several such dances they went back upstairs. Gina could feel the tension in Quentin, and see from the deepening lines on his face that his emotions were running dangerously high. Her own pulse was racing, but as much with fear as passion, for she didn't look forward to the part she must play. Yet what other alternative did she have, with a partner so wholly without integrity?

Even so, she smiled at him in the lift, a teasing, slightly seductive smile that brought a dull flush to his hard cheeks and his mouth swiftly ravaging on hers. 'Gina,' he groaned, as the lift stopped.

In their suite he dragged her to him, one of his arms never having left her narrow waist. Now his hands and mouth combined in an assault that played havoc with her senses. As she clung to him feverishly, he lifted her, carrying her swiftly through to the bedroom. Laying her on the bed, he ruthlessly disposed of their clothes.

'I want you,' he groaned. 'I've waited so long, Gina.' His hands were still on her and he slid them completely around her, his gentle kiss turning to fire.

Helplessly she gave in, assuring her dazed mind that it would only be for a moment. One brief moment before she rejected him. His mouth devoured hers with urgent kisses, his hands even more urgent on her throbbing breast, and she couldn't control her own vibrant response.

Lifting her a little away from him, his mouth moved over her, exploring with devastating thoroughness before he again moulded her to him, groaning thick words of protest as she just managed to evade his determination to possess her completely.

'Gina . . .' his voice was hoarse, 'you want me just as much, so stop struggling.' His mouth came down over hers, warm and sensuous, denying any harshness. 'Gina,' he said thickly, as if wryly pleading his own cause, 'I'm going mad, wanting you so much.'

Something strange stirred in Gina then and her body tingled as she wrapped urgent arms around him. Never could she remember wanting anything so much. Everything inside her seemed to be breaking up as their bodies burned and melted together in growing excitement. In another second it might be too late, but nothing she had ever done had taken as much effort. Bemused, in a fog of passion, her mind reeled. If she was hurting him she was about to hurt herself even more. This she fully understood as she suddenly pushed forcibly away from him, twisting desperately to escape his suddenly smothering weight.

'No,' she cried, 'Quentin, don't . . .' Her exhausted

whisper, as she fought to be free of him, sounded deafening to her ears. 'Let me go, Quentin. I hate you!'

It seemed he would ignore her struggles, putting them down to a girl's natural fears, but her last utterance made him pause long enough for her to pull herself from his arms. Her words, she thought hysterically, might have had the same effect as an icy shower.

For a moment he didn't move, although he still breathed hard. Then he said slowly, 'Gina, I do realise you haven't slept with a man before. I was going to be gentle.'

'It's not that!' she gasped unevenly. 'I don't want you near me because of what I've discovered.' Oddly defensive, her voice rose. 'You're a thief and a liar, and I won't have you touching me!'

Eyes narrowed, he stared down at her, but made no attempt to prevent her from covering her nakedness with a sheet. 'This seems to be more than normal virginal fright,' he said harshly at last, 'Perhaps you'd better explain.'

Feeling chilled by his quick transition from passion to coldness, even if it only matched her own, Gina watched apprehensively as he swung off the bed to reach for a short robe. As he shrugged into it he turned to look at her again, his dark brows lifting grimly. 'Well? he prompted savagely. 'I'm waiting.'

Because she felt she had wasted enough time, Gina's words tumbled angrily over themselves. 'You're in financial difficulties and took money from my grandfather to settle your debts. And he's having to sell his London home because of it. You cheated to get it by making him believe you loved me. You were aware that he blamed himself that my parents' marriage had a bad start and was determined it wouldn't happen to me. You played on these feelings in order to get what you wanted.'

'Will you shut up!' Quentin snarled. Then moderating

his tones with obvious difficulty, he asked tersely, 'Who
told you this?'

Her sudden, wild hope that it wasn't true died quickly
when she thought of the evidence. 'Never mind who told
me,' she replied stonily. 'It wasn't my grandfather, and
he doesn't know I know. Can you deny about the
money?'

Briefly he hesitated before shaking his head, like a man
in a bad dream. 'I don't intend denying anything,' he
exclaimed with soft violence.

Somehow Gina had hoped he would, but as he didn't
she forced down all feelings but anger. 'Why do you think
I wouldn't go anywhere but here for my honeymoon?
Even this, I suppose, will have to be paid for with
someone else's money.'

Quentin straightened away from her and she had never
seen his face so white. He looked dreadful, even his eyes
were like burning black coals. Suddenly her torment was
so great she could scarcely endure it.

From a distance she heard him asking bleakly, 'Charles
told me you loved me. It isn't true?'

'If it was,' she choked, shocked that Charles had so
betrayed her, 'you've certainly killed it. All I feel now is
hate. As soon as possible I'm going to leave you!'

Quentin's laughter was harsh and mirthless, making
her shrink. 'For years I've lived with your hate, Gina.
I'm too used to it to let it worry me. You'll continue as
my wife—and to live with me, for as long as I choose.'

'We'll see about that!' she muttered.

His mouth tightened ominously in the hardness of his
face. 'I suppose your convincing little display of passion
tonight was all pretence? A desire for revenge?'

Her cheeks burned and she had to drop her eyes.
'Don't you think you deserved something?'

'Not that kind of punishment,' he retorted harshly, 'but
maybe I should be grateful you weren't more subtle—you

might have kept me in suspense for days if you'd chosen
to play the young, nervous bride.'

'I couldn't pretend that with a thief!'

'Be careful!' His tone was suddenly violent, and she
had a frightening suspicion he would like to strangle her,
but instead he turned and strode from the room. 'Goodnight and sweet dreams,' was all he said, but this so savagely that the door shook as he slammed it behind him.

Gina wasn't sure if he went out or slept in the small
dressing room adjoining. She was sure she had never felt
so unhappy in her life. Her half awakened body gave her
no peace and her mind less. Would she have felt worse,
she wondered, if she had let Quentin make love to her
and pretended to know nothing of his guilty secrets?

She was so long falling asleep that she slept in and
woke with dismay to find it was nine, and no sign of
Quentin anywhere. Hastily she scrambled out of bed to
have a shower and dress. She had just finished when he
arrived.

While she tried not to look at him, his gaunt, grim face
caught her gaze and she couldn't look away. This morning he looked every one of his thirty-six years—he would
have passed easily for forty. Swallowing a swift despair,
she averted her eyes. This must be what guilt and worry
did for a man. He must be terrified she intended betraying him.

She felt bitter to hear herself reassuring him, but
couldn't seem to help it. 'You can stop worrying about
the money. I won't tell Grandfather I know, in case you
think I've changed my mind about that. Nor will I mention it to anyone else.'

Grimly Quentin took in the beautiful picture she made
in her light summer dress. His eyes glittered, as he replied
abruptly, 'Very magnanimous of you.'

'Perhaps I'm thinking of myself.' Before his insolent
sarcasm her softer feelings faded. 'In the eyes of other

people I'm still your wife. I only hope the law doesn't catch up with you.'

'Don't worry,' he retorted tightly, 'at least you can be sure of that.'

Coldly she shrugged. 'We'll be going home today?'

'Ah, yes,' he ran a thoughtful hand around his chin, which she saw in spite of his haggard appearance was smoothly shaven, 'you can't bear to think that your grandfather's money is paying for all this?' Suddenly, vindictively he swung around on her, grasping her shaking shoulders. 'Well, you can damned well stick it out for a week. If you could get through the marriage ceremony with so much hate in your heart then a few days here should be easy.'

Beneath his hurting hands Gina went cold. Put like that she seemed almost worse than he was, but just as long as he was sure it was hatred in her heart she could at least save her pride. He didn't seem to understand she had lost her respect for him. Or, if he did, he didn't care.

'Where did you go last night?' she whispered, feeling she had to know.

'Never mind,' he returned shortly. 'I wasn't lonely. No man of my questionable character ever is. Now,' he asked, abruptly letting go of her, 'are you coming down for breakfast?'

'I may as well,' she agreed dejectedly. How was she to get through the next few days, if he insisted on staying?

He did, and, as she had suspected she might, she suffered. Quentin turned himself into a polite and impersonal guide. When it came to seeing the sights, he made sure she had nothing to complain of. He knew Vienna well and took her to all the most famous places. For hours of each day they toured until she was almost physically exhausted, and at nights fell into a deep, drugged sleep, which was probably what he intended.

During the day he escorted her through numerous

museums and churches, and when she grew tired of these they explored parks and gardens. Then he would take her shopping. Shopping in Vienna was very expensive, but the shops were stocked with lovely things. At first Gina enjoyed looking around them, until Quentin began loading her with extravagant presents. It didn't take her long to realise he was doing this deliberately, but to her it seemed the height of folly. It wasn't his own money he was spending, it was money belonging to her grandfather and heaven knew how many other people, and she was sure he had no right to be spending it this way! She was puzzled that her angry anxiety, instead of restraining him, seemed to be bringing a perverse satisfaction.

She bought her own presents to take home herself, from her own money. From one of the shops along the Karntnerstrasse she bought her grandfather a model of one of the famous Riding School horses. Of all the places they had visited, she had enjoyed the Spanish Riding School best. She had loved the elegant Lippizzaner horses with their equally elegant, uniformed riders who could control them so superbly. They had visited the stables, too, in the Stallburg, Reitschulgasse, opposite the Riding School. Each horse had its name on a board above its stall, telling you when it was born, and she had been especially interested in the shining harness hanging over the side. She had caught the only flicker of amusement she was to see in the whole week in Quentin's eyes as he had to almost drag her away.

If things had been different she would have been thrilled by her visit to Vienna, which had once been the capital of an empire stretching from the Balkans to Berlin. So many nationalities had lived there and left something of themselves behind, but she was unable to decide whether the atmosphere was sad or gay. The one or two Viennese whom she managed to talk to in shops hadn't been able to decide either, so she supposed it must depend on circumstance. If Quentin and she had been a normal honeymoon couple she might have had no difficulty in finding the city extremely gay.

The evenings were the worst, for always after an early dinner Quentin saw her to her room, then bade her a polite goodnight. Where he went afterwards she didn't know, but once, when, unable to sleep at four in the morning, she had peeped stealthily into his dressing room he hadn't been there. He must have been out, but she couldn't tell by his coolly enigmatic demeanour next morning whether he had enjoyed himself or not.

He was always a polite stranger, so much so that Gina sighed with relief at the end of the week when he told her they were going home. At least, at Briarly, there would be something to do and Quentin would be in London most of the time. There wouldn't be his constant presence to torment her and make her conscious of her aching needs.

CHAPTER NINE

THE journey back was uneventful, and as they neared Briarly Quentin said curtly, 'I'd rather you didn't mention anything about money to my mother. It would only upset her needlessly.'

'I had no intention of saying anything to her,' Gina retorted, then heard herself pleading impulsively, 'Quentin, couldn't you pay the money back?'

'No,' he replied brusquely, 'I could not.'

Couldn't or wouldn't? Noting the hardness of his jaw, Gina sighed. He didn't appreciate her disapproval, but surely he didn't expect her to condone what he had done? On the other hand it grieved her that she had so little influence over him. If he had loved her he might have been willing to mend his ways—to do anything to regain her respect.

Attempting to hide her hurt, she spoke sharply. 'There doesn't seem much sense in your mother looking for a house of her own now. She may as well stay on at Briarly.'

'If you like,' he agreed coldly.

'And I can go back to my old room. It's very comfortable.'

'You'll sleep with me!'

'Sleep with you?' Shocked surprise swung her around to stare at him with angry, resentful eyes. 'Why?'

Cold mockery, and something else, lay in the idle glance he flicked over her. 'If that's a question, why not?'

'You know why not,' she said fiercely.

'Yes, I know,' she thought for a moment he sounded despondent, 'but we can't do anything about that. Perhaps you should remember how you promised to take me for better or worse—then you mightn't feel such a sense of disappointment.'

Gina gazed straight in front. 'But I didn't promise to sleep with you.'

'Now you're being childish.' He sounded indifferent, but there was no softening of his expression. 'There's a room at the west side of the house with twin beds. Twin beds, my dear,' he mocked, 'in case you believe I'm not thinking of you, provide the ideal solution. No one can be quite sure what's going on.'

'But they're in the same room!' she hissed, scarcely following his logic.

'Don't worry,' he said cynically, 'I won't ask anything of you except that you sleep there. I'm not interested in anything else.'

'Not from me.'

'Certainly not from you.'

She supposed she deserved that and might have expected it, but she hadn't been prepared for the depth of pain inside her. Quentin hadn't attempted to touch her since that first night of their honeymoon, and he'd had enough opportunity. He was unlikely to begin making advances now. His pride alone would keep him at a distance. Stealing a puzzled glance at his aloof, arrogant profile, Gina failed to understand why neither the apparent failure of his business or her scorn had managed to humble him. Then again, how would she feel to see him down? Never in her whole life could she recall him being any other than he was now. While despairing of what she considered softness, she wondered if she could bear to see him humbled and completely defeated.

At Briarly they found Mrs Hurst too taken up with her own affairs to ask why they had cut short their honeymoon. Her personal assistant, as she liked to call her, had left without warning, over a silly disagreement she had had with Mrs Worth.

With his habitual cynicism, Quentin watched as Gina made futile attempts to calm his mother, and suddenly incensed by his indifference, she offered to help Mrs Hurst herself. Speaking almost simultaneously with Quentin, who said carelessly that they would get someone else, Gina offered her services and was gratefully accepted. Ignoring Quentin's quick frown, she decided it would give her something to do, and be one way of cutting expenses. If he wouldn't make a start in this direction, then she must! It was surely dishonest to afford oneself luxuries on borrowed money.

Matthews had taken their luggage upstairs, after removing it from the car, and she asked Mrs Hurst to excuse her while she changed for dinner. It was still early, but she wanted to ring Bourne Court, to tell them she was home.

Quentin followed her up. 'I'd better show you our room.' He spoke so tersely Gina guessed he was still not pleased about her offer to work for his mother.

She hadn't been to this part of the house before and gazed doubtfully around the comfortable bedroom to which he silently escorted her. It was beautifully decorated in quiet pastel colours, but in her present mood she would have been more pleased with an attic.

As if guessing her thoughts, he said sarcastically, 'Don't let your sense of economy run away with you. As we still have it we may as well use it. Secondhand furniture has little value.'

'It might please your creditors better than nothing!'

He made no reply, but a quick glance confirmed that he didn't trust himself to. Quaking, Gina averted her eyes to the twin beds, finding little to reassure her there. Each of them looked as large as a normal double. There was nothing cramped about them to drive Quentin away, should he decide to share one with her.

'There's a dressing-room,' he announced abruptly, speaking at last, and surprising her, 'I'll sleep there.'

Confused, and oddly ashamed of herself, she had to force herself to mutter, 'I suppose, if you do decide to get rid of me, now you have my grandfather's money, it will be easier if you don't sleep here.'

He came so close she could feel the warmth from his body, she could also see the coldness in his eyes. 'Don't push your luck too far, Gina, I'm highly inflammable material right now. I don't want to hear you mention money—not *that* money—ever again!'

If she had been going to argue, his tormenting nearness made her change her mind. He could make her quiver just by looking at her. She knew it and so, unfortunately, did he!

'I'm going to give my grandfather a ring and then get ready for dinner,' she gasped. 'If you'll excuse me?'

'Don't let me stop you,' he retorted, jerking away from her. 'I can take a hint, and I'm sure you won't want my help.'

'No,' she agreed icily.

'Such a cool little voice,' he mocked, his eyes taunting on the agitated heave of her breasts. 'Just think if things had been different between us. I could have helped you undress. We might even have shared the same bath—it's big enough, and I could have scrubbed your back, and other places. You might even have done the same for me.'

'Will you get out!' Her face and voice both flamed with anger and heat. The deliberately jeering curve of his mouth provoked her into adding unwisely, 'If I ever do that for a man it won't be you!'

This halted his leisurely departure. He turned in the doorway, his glance slicing into her. 'That's one more thing. While you're still married to me, I won't have you going out with other men, so when the good Richard or Felix, or whoever, present sympathetic shoulders to cry on, you'd better ignore them.'

'I'll do . . .' she had been going to say 'what I like', but

Quentin was gone before she could finish, leaving her staring angrily at the closed door.

In spite of the cooling effect of anger, she had some difficulty in controlling all the sensuous thoughts he had aroused and pounced on the telephone as if it were a lifeline. Suddenly she felt almost desperate for the soothing sanity of her grandfather's voice.

It came almost as a shock to discover neither Charles nor Liza at home. The housekeeper informed Gina that they wouldn't be back for at least another two weeks. When Gina asked if they were in London, she was told no, that the London house had been sold. They were with a friend, on his yacht. It had been an unexpected invitation.

Oh, well, Gina sighed, squashing down her own selfish regrets, it was what they both needed. They wouldn't be away that long and a holiday would do them good.

Dinner proved for Gina a long, dreary hour that dragged. It also provided some humiliating moments. Quentin's mother enquired belatedly why they had returned so soon from their honeymoon, and Quentin murmured something about urgent business.

'But you said you might be away for weeks!'

'We got fed up,' he replied curtly, with no regard for Gina's feelings, or Myra's pricked ears.

Wholly aware of Mrs Hurst's surprise and Myra's startled interest, which almost made her drop the iced sweet she was serving, Gina sank beneath a sea of embarrassment. How dared Quentin do this to her!

'Or perhaps it was because Gina's clairvoyant?' she heard him suggesting suavely, without humour. 'She must have sensed you were in need of help.'

'Well, it's very kind of her to offer to help me.' Mrs Hurst sounded gratified but looked slightly bewildered.

'I won't bother with coffee.' His voice suddenly leashed, Quentin rose. 'I'm going to work in my study.

I'll leave you to discuss Gina's duties.'

By the end of the week Gina felt tired and not a little
fed up with the whole situation. Quentin continued treat-
ing her like a stranger, but while she had expected him to
stay in London, which might have afforded her some
relief, he came home each evening, and once appeared
for lunch—an unheard-of thing. His mother, on the other
hand, seemed to forget she was Quentin's wife and began
ordering her around much as she had done when Gina
had worked for her before. Not that Gina minded terribly. Through the day she was too busy to think and by
evening she was often too exhausted to. She grew used to
Quentin sleeping next door, but he complained that she
tossed and turned so much she kept him awake.

One afternoon, when she had managed to escape, she
went riding and met Felix Duke, who begged her to
come and have a cup of tea with him.

'I haven't seen you since you were married,' he said
ruefully, his eyes on Gina's lovely young face, 'and I
missed you a lot during the year you were away. You'll
have to take pity on me.'

Gina laughed, refusing to take him seriously, but said
she would love a cup of tea.

Felix laughed, too, but his eyes darkened. 'I don't
know why I allowed Quentin to steal you the way he did,
but then he always was a fast worker.'

'With women, you mean?'

'They seem to like him. Of course,' he added hastily, 'it
will be different now he's married.'

'I hope so,' she replied lightly, but felt the smile leave
her lips.

'I expect personal charm and financial genius are an
unbeatable combination,' Felix sighed, quite without ran-
cour, 'and Quentin has both.'

'Financial genius?' Gina glanced at him sharply.

Felix was tolerant. 'Your husband's reputation is well
known, you know.'

Gina hadn't known. At least, she hadn't been sure, for she'd never taken a great deal of interest in that side of Quentin's life or enquired too closely into his business talents. She had been vaguely aware that he was considered brilliant. A quick frown knitted her brow as something elusive came to confuse and tantalise her, but before she had time to define it they arrived on Felix's doorstep and her bewilderment was forgotten.

It was later than she had intended it should be when she returned to Briarly and rushed up to her room to change for dinner. She found herself wishing that she and Quentin had been an ordinary couple in a small house of their own, so that being late for dinner wouldn't have mattered.

To her relief there was no sign of him and she flung off her clothes and dived under the shower. She hadn't seemed to be there more than a minute when she distinctly heard a door open sharply. Peculiarly beset by apprehension, she leapt out of the cubicle and grabbed her silky robe. Without stopping to dry herself she pulled it around her wet body as she went back to the bedroom.

Quentin was there, as she had somehow feared he would be, with just a towel thrust around his middle. His chest was bare and she couldn't recall seeing him like this before, not even at the hotel where they had spent their honeymoon. There, on the one occasion when she might have done, it had been too dark to see. Or had she been too blinded by desire and uncertainty to see him properly?

For days, now, he had scarcely spoken to her, and strangely she resented this as much as she did his watch-dog attitude. 'If anything's wrong——' she knew she spoke insolently, 'I'm not interested. I'd like to get ready for dinner, so would you please get out of my room.'

'I'll leave when I'm ready.' He eyed the defiant pinkness in her cheeks narrowly, obviously holding on to his own temper with difficulty.

The wet from the shower soaking her robe was becoming uncomfortable, as were the flickers of heat which ran crazily through her limbs as her eyes were drawn against her will to the powerful breadth of his bare shoulders and the thick covering of dark hair below them. It appeared to run right down past his navel. Swallowing hard, she dragged her eyes back to his face. Perhaps if she changed her tactics he might be willing to go?

'I'm sorry,' she murmured, 'I—I didn't mean to sound aggressive, but you know how your mother dislikes being kept waiting.'

'Whose fault will that be tonight?' Quentin asked, moving so near that the sharp, clean scent of his skin filled her nostrils.

A sudden flicker of intuition warned her he knew exactly where she had been, but she tried to bluff it out. 'I realise I have only myself to blame, but I got held up.'

'With Duke?'

So her intuition had been right? He did know. Well, she wouldn't try to deny it. 'You sound as though I'd committed a crime! I only accepted a cup of tea.'

'I asked you not to see him.'

'I didn't meet him deliberately, if that's what you're thinking.'

He didn't answer at once, but after a moment he said curtly, 'How you meet him is irrelevant. Going to his house is another matter. His mother is away.'

'So what?' she interrupted swiftly, her nerves almost at breaking point. It just had to be funny, that while he attacked her about other men the only man she could think of was him! Didn't he know what his nearness was doing to her!

'Have you slept with him yet?' Quentin's snarling query made her gasp, for she hadn't expected him to have thought she would have sunk as low as that.

'No, I have not!' Meeting his grey, contemptuous eyes, her own grew hot with anger. 'But I almost wish I had done.'

'Why?' he jeered. 'Aren't you learning to live with frustration?'

'How—how dare you!' she cried. Against his leashed sarcasm her fury was a livid, outgoing thing, threatening to shatter her to pieces if it couldn't find release. To smack his mocking face with her hand wouldn't do. Wildly she grasped the glass vase of flowers behind her, flinging them at him. He ducked, and instead of hitting him, the vase crashed into the bathroom door behind him, breaking to a thousand glittering pieces.

Instantly, as she would have turned and run, he caught hold of her, his anger mounting savagely as he brought her brutally to him. One of his hands tangled in her hair to drag her head back, while his other arm went around her so tightly she couldn't move. She could scarcely even breathe, he held her so closely. Then, as if determined to inflict more punishment, his mouth took hers, crushing open her shaking lips, searching, demanding, no tenderness behind the driving force of his kiss.

Ever since that first night of their honeymoon, subconsciously she had yearned for this, and the damped-down fires inside her refused to be denied such instant refuelling. If she struggled at first, she soon melted and burned as Quentin thrust her robe back until there was nothing between them. The harsh insistence of his mouth hurt but was arousing a storm of passion, a sensuous hunger which threatened to evade control as he moulded her ever closer. They could neither of them seem to get near enough. Gina felt the imprint of his hand crushing her taut breasts, the strength of his limbs pressing forcibly against her limbs.

'Don't move,' he groaned, as they gasped for breath, their breathing quickening urgently. 'I could take you now.'

And how could she stop him? Did she want to?

The battering on the door was no louder than her heartbeats. Quentin lifted his head, releasing her suddenly. Gina's hand went blindly to her burning cheeks as he pulled up his slipping towel and left her to see who was there.

It was Myra, apprehensive but curious. Gina was relieved that Quentin's tallness concealed her from Myra's darting eyes.

'Your mother thought she heard a terrible crash, Mr Quentin. She sent me to see . . .'

Above her still erratic breathing, Gina heard Quentin's reply. 'My wife slipped with the flower vase, Myra. Perhaps you'd come back later and clear it up?' His voice was unbelievably steady.

'Couldn't you think of anything better than that?' Gina exclaimed helplessly. 'What sort of wife will they think me?'

'I'm beginning to wonder myself.' Turning, as Myra left, he regarded her so coolly she gasped. He made no attempt to come near her again.

Because she had to try desperately to achieve even a modicum of composure, she envied Quentin his immediate control. She hated him for it, as it seemed to demonstrate clearly how little she really disturbed him. It induced her to fall pleading at his feet, but for her pride's sake she chose to attack him. 'You promised not to touch me.'

'I didn't promise anything,' his eyes narrowed on her white, strained face, 'but I have no wish to struggle with your hate. An unwilling bride doesn't appeal to me.'

'You know why I can't be anything else,' she faltered, close to tears.

'We won't go into that,' he cut in tersely. 'It's not important, and, as you pointed out a few regrettable minutes ago, we will be late for dinner if we don't hurry.'

A few days after this, as though they hadn't enough problems, Jenkins the groom told Gina he was leaving. He was having trouble with his wife, who refused to leave London, and who threatened to go off with another man if Jim didn't find another job in an area she liked. As he wanted to leave immediately Gina, seeing this suddenly as a further means of saving money, made no attempt to stop him and, without consulting Quentin, said she was quite willing to take over. It would also be a chance to see more of her beloved horses, and she could still continue to help Mrs Hurst.

Quentin had to know, of course, because, for one thing, there were various documents to be sent on. What Gina didn't learn was that Quentin delivered the relevant matter himself and told Jenkins exactly what he thought of him leaving without giving proper notice.

He found Gina at the stables when he returned that evening, but he didn't say where he had been. Absently, he rubbed Hector's enquiring nose. 'I'll get on to the unemployment people first thing in the morning.'

'No need.' Gina was cleaning tack, which she had decided was looking neglected. She kept her head bent over it. 'I can manage, like I used to. Anyway, you mightn't find it easy to get someone else. There isn't a house.'

There were two cottages, but the gardener lived in one and Mrs Worth had the other. 'I'm having another one built,' Quentin replied. 'I had plans drawn up and passed some time ago. In the meantime, a new groom can always lodge in the village, as Jenkins did.'

'But, Quentin!' Disconcerted, Gina forgot to keep her head down. Lifting it now to stare at him, she stammered, 'You can't go to all that—I mean, you can't possibly afford to go to all that expense now.'

'Gina!' His voice hardened warningly.

'I know!' she retorted tautly, her face paling. 'I haven't to mention it, but how can I say nothing when you continue to spend money you haven't got so recklessly!'

He looked as though he would like to have killed her, but suddenly changed his mind. His face almost as taut as her own, he said grimly, 'Please yourself what you do, but

don't begin complaining when you run out of strength.'
With visible effort he spoke more gently. 'Gina, is it any
good asking you to reconsider?'

Abruptly she shook her head. 'I'll do what I think is
best. I don't need your advice.'

Grimly he thrust a hand under her chin, turning her
face up to his before she could move. 'What happened to
the young girl who was always seeking my advice? Begging for it many a night, almost before I had time to get
out of my car. You were always a headstrong child, but
you liked me well enough then. I was forever falling over
you. Now you won't listen to anything I say and you
don't even like me any more.'

Gina's throat went dry, for she seemed to sense behind
his anger a great area of bleakness. Wouldn't it be so easy
to throw her arms around him and forget everything else,
if there hadn't been so much distrust and lack of respect
between them. But a lack of respect might kill even lust,
eventually!

Unhappily she whispered, 'How can I come to you any
more when there are things we can't talk about?'

'Ah, yes. My dishonesty,' he sneered, his grip on her
soft throat tightening before he almost threw her away
from him. Turning on his heel, he retorted harshly, his
eyes black as he left her, 'I'm quite aware there are things
you can't forgive, Gina. I only hope you don't expect me
to forgive you more easily when the time comes.'

'You could help with the horses!' she called after him
weakly, scarcely taking in what he was saying. She hadn't
meant to plead, but suddenly she couldn't bear to see him
go with so much violence on his face. If only she could
make him understand!

'I might——' he paused, his mouth curling in the old
familiar way she had learnt to fear. 'Blanche rang, just
before I came out to come here, actually. She's coming
over in the morning for a ride.'

'But where's her own horse, the black one? I——'

'Yes?' Quentin prompted shortly. Then, as she hesitated, he asked curiously, 'When did you see her on that?'

Wishing she hadn't mentioned it, she replied uncertainly, 'A few weeks ago.'

Quentin frowned. 'Her brother doesn't have it now. He sold it.'

He seemed remarkably clued up on Blanche's mounts and her family. Well, a little more torture couldn't make all that much difference to the ultimate pain, and it wasn't as if Quentin wouldn't suffer too. To have to spend a few hours in the company of a girl he had wanted to marry, and the one he had been forced to, for financial reasons, wouldn't surely provide him with a great deal of pleasure either.

It made Gina angry, but more unhappy than she had bargained for, to find herself trailing after Blanche and Quentin next morning, much as she had used to do. Quentin had even kissed Blanche lightly on the cheek when she had turned up at the stables after the work was all done and the horses standing ready. Gina, who had been up since dawn, hadn't received from him so much as a kind glance.

When Felix appeared over the brow of the hill and offered his unfailing hospitality, she merely felt irritated. She knew she was being unfair, but she wanted to refuse it.

Not so Blanche. Flushed by Quentin's flattering attention and his obvious neglect of his wife, she gave him a brilliant smile, edging so close to him that their thighs touched as she caught his arm. 'Come on, darling, say yes to the poor man.'

Quentin, returning her smile, if not quite so brilliantly, had obviously no intention of saying no, and Gina had to endure what stretched into an hour of having to sit and watch Blanche flirt quite shamelessly with her not uncooperative husband. After a while Felix must have imagined this gave him a legitimate right to do the same thing and turned his attention to Gina, who felt compelled for her pride's sake to make some show of responding.

As Felix settled too near her, however, on a low couch, Quentin immediately rose to his feet, announcing that it was time they were going. If the smouldering anger in his eyes didn't explain why, it must have given even the most disinterested onlooker some idea.

Gina, her resentment increasing, felt so miserable that she galloped in front on the way home, so she wouldn't have to watch Quentin and Blanche again. She realised they were following at a more leisurely pace, but after she had unsaddled and rubbed down there was still no sign of them. Feeling near to angry tears, she decided to go back to the house and leave them to manage themselves. Perhaps Quentin wouldn't be so pleased with Blanche when he found he had everything to do for her.

Gina was in her room when she remembered how Quentin was always accusing her of being childish. Did her behaviour, this morning, merely confirm it? For a moment she paused, her hands on her aching head. If he could read the state of her mind, he would know the sweeping waves of emotion which constantly threatened to take over were far from childish! He couldn't read her mind, though, so he wouldn't know, and it was better that he shouldn't. But to prevent this she might be wiser to return to the stables, where she could pretend to be waiting for him and Blanche, indifferently.

It wasn't until she reached the stable door that she realised they were back, as she recognised Hector's welcoming whinny, but if this startled her it startled her even more to find Blanche in Quentin's arms. True, Quentin's big body concealed Blanche's, but nothing could hide the fact that her two hands were linked behind his neck and that Quentin's dark head was bent. With a stifled cry Gina ran back the way she had come.

This incident unnerved her so thoroughly that during the following days she often wondered how long she could go on. The only relief she could find was in work, and she worked until she was so tired she could almost forget how she had felt on finding Blanche in the stables with Quentin. As she grew paler and thinner, Quentin had every appearance of a man driven near desperation, yet she couldn't think of anything to say to him. If she were to offer him his freedom he would only refuse, as he must still need her grandfather's help and support.

She thought about her grandfather a lot, and when he rang after lunch one day to say he was home again, she felt so glad to hear his voice she could scarcely speak.

'If you can spare an hour I'd love to see you,' he said.

'I'll be right over,' she managed to reply before she rang off.

Charles was waiting when she arrived, and again she felt weepy as she hugged him and they went arm in arm into the drawing-room. Not wanting to worry him by being over-emotional, Gina asked how he was, then began teasing him lightly about always being away.

'Well, don't blame me this time,' he laughed. 'It was your husband.'

'Quentin?'

He was surprised at her surprise. 'He arranged it, didn't he tell you? He insisted a change would do me good.'

'How kind of him!'

'Yes, wasn't it?' Charles didn't detect her sarcasm, obviously because he wasn't looking for it. 'I must say I feel much better, so does your aunt.'

'Where is Aunt Liza?' asked Gina.

Charles grunted. 'Gone to see her friend, Mrs what's-her-name, at the other side of Dorking. The one who's an invalid and doesn't get out much. Liza's gone to tell her all about it. Thought it would cheer her up.'

'I see.' Gina was disappointed.

Charles defended his sister. 'We didn't expect you would be back from your honeymoon. If she'd known, I'm sure she wouldn't have gone out. When I rang Briarly I expected to speak to Lydia.'

Gina endeavoured to remain composed. 'We only stayed in Vienna a week. Which reminds me,' she tried to laugh, 'I have some presents for you and forgot to bring them with me.'

Her grandfather didn't reply. Outside it was raining, and to escape getting wet Gina had rushed into the house when she had arrived. Looking at her, Charles was seeing her properly for the first time. He seemed suddenly startled by her pallor. 'You look like a ghost, child. Aren't you happy?'

Hastily she deviated, not wishing him to guess, 'Quentin's groom left and I'm doing his job, and Mrs Hurst's maid left and I'm helping her, but I'm quite all right.'

'But why?' Charles was clearly bewildered. 'You're far too thin without doing all that! I'd like to know what Quentin's thinking about!'

Suddenly Gina had an urgent inclination to defend Quentin, which must be strange, when she hated him so. But she hated it more that Charles should believe Quentin had simply accepted his money without any intention of economising or paying it back. Maybe she could give him a hint that they were trying.

Swallowing painfully, she forced herself to smile. 'It's— well, it's a sort of economy measure. We're trying to re-trench.'

'Retrench?' He frowned, mulling the word over. 'When people retrench it means they're cutting back, trying to save money?'

'Yes.'

There was an odd silence. Glancing quickly at her grandfather's grave face, she hoped he was beginning to understand, without her having to be more explicit. Maybe Quentin didn't deserve to be defended like this, but she felt driven to do it.

'Do you mean to say,' Charles asked slowly, 'that Quentin needs to save that kind of money?'

At once, Gina saw her mistake. Now Charles would imagine he hadn't given Quentin enough, that they were still short and she was begging indirectly for more. Somehow she had to stop him offering them more, which was what he clearly intended. She must do something to remove the almost anguished expression from his face. And there was only one way.

'Grandfather,' she whispered, her eyes full of despair, 'I know!'

'You know?' he exclaimed harshly. 'You know what?'

'About the money.'

'Quentin said he wouldn't tell you!'

'I guessed.'

Before her very eyes, Charles' face crumpled. He seemed suddenly to grow old. Collapsing on to the chair behind him, he buried his face in his hands. 'Quentin shouldn't have made me take the money,' he muttered heavily. 'He should have left me to face the music. I'll always be grateful, but it was wrong of me to let him settle my debts, especially when it's meant he's had to go short himself, and you're having to suffer.'

'Grandfather!' No less disturbed, Gina stared at him, a terrible constriction in her throat. 'I thought it was Quentin who had borrowed from you?'

'No,' he shook his head sadly, without understanding her dilemma. 'I was a fool. I gambled unwisely and lost. You see, I've always refused to believe I was getting older. I liked to travel—keep up with much younger people. Thank goodness it's never been women,' he said, with grim wryness, 'but I've tried about everything else. When the chance of turning my million, shall we say, into millions, came up, I took it, and I've only myself to blame that I failed.'

'And then what:'

'Quentin had heard, or guessed, and of course I couldn't deny it.'

Gina saw Charles's hands were trembling and put her own hands gently over his. After a few seconds he gave her a grateful glance and continued. 'He offered to help me out, for your sake, and I'm ashamed to admit I almost fell over myself to accept. I sold the London house and some land, but that was all the concession he would allow me to make. He said he would never miss the money, and I believed him.'

'Oh, Grandfather,' Gina was almost weeping, 'you can believe him! It's me . . . If you've been a fool, I've been one as well. Someone told me, you see, that it was Quentin who'd borrowed money from you.'

'No, never!' Charles was shocked. 'Who was it?'

'Blanche Edgar.'

'She must have heard something in the City—these things get about.' Again he frowned. 'Has it made much difference to you? You said you were having to retrench.'

'No, of course not,' she lied. 'I thought I was helping Quentin by trying to economise, but now I know the truth there'll be no need.'

The casual way she tried to speak reassured him, and he sighed. 'In the ordinary way, I wouldn't have asked Quentin not to tell you, but I've had you for such a short time. I couldn't seem to bear the thought of you thinking badly of me, but Quentin promised you would never hear of it from him. One day, of course, you would have had to know, because I can't leave you what I've no longer got. Technically, you understand, everything I have belongs to your husband.'

CHAPTER TEN

GINA had no clear recollection of how she reached home that afternoon. Her grandfather, strangely enough, seemed happier when she left than he had done when she arrived, but she was aware that this was because he no longer feared she would discover his guilty secret and despise him for it. That she did know and forgave him had obviously removed a great burden from his mind.

Gina wished that she, too, could have felt happier. It was certainly a relief to know Quentin hadn't taken Charles's money, but this didn't alter the fact that she had believed he had done, and that it was unlikely he would ever forgive her for her lack of trust.

A hundred times between Bourne Court and Briarly, she wondered how she could ever have thought Quentin capable of stealing, for this, she frankly admitted, was what she had practically accused him of. Of course other men as brilliant as Quentin had failed; she had heard him say, himself, that in business one could never be absolutely certain of anything, but she ought to have had more faith in him.

And, apart from faith, hadn't there been other things which should have made her doubt her own foolish convictions? If Quentin's financial empire had collapsed there would have been plenty about it in the newspapers. He couldn't possibly have carried on as though nothing had happened. A man of his intelligence wouldn't have wanted to. She ought to have disregarded Blanche's statement that Quentin's downfall was common knowledge when no one else appeared to know of it. Felix Duke, for one, would have known as he had many connections in

the City, but always he had only praise for Quentin's
infallibility. If only, Gina thought desperately, she had
been sensible enough not to listen to gossip.

She would have to apologise, but she suspected it
would make little difference. Quentin might only despise
her more. However, whether he did or not, she would
have to make her confession, and after dinner, if he would
see her alone, would perhaps be the best time to speak to
him about it.

Despairingly, as she dressed for dinner later, she found
herself taking extra care over her appearance. As if that
would make any difference! But after washing and drying
her hair she made sure that this and her face and hands
were beyond reproach, never having quite been able to
forget how Quentin used to be forever telling her she
looked far from clean. Yet his former disparagement
seemed nothing, this evening, compared with her own
discreditable conduct! For the first time she believed he
had more to forgive her for than she had him. Hers was
the greater sin.

Trying to shut out the memory of the curt remark he
had once made about not expecting him to forgive her so
easily, she trailed unhappily downstairs. Her palms were
damp with apprehension and she felt slightly unsteady on
her feet, but otherwise she was in control of herself. Deliberately she steered her chaotic thoughts away from her
charade of a honeymoon, the wasted opportunities, which
made her want to break down openly and weep.

Quentin was late home, he still hadn't arrived as she
entered the drawing-room. There wouldn't be time to
speak to him now before dinner, and if she waited upstairs
she might be tempted to try.

When he did put in an appearance, she was pouring
his mother a glass of sherry and filling one for herself.
Thinking of her coming ordeal, she turned to gaze at
him, but wasn't able to raise even a small smile. She did
manage to ask meekly if she could get him anything.

'I'll get my own,' he said lightly, casting her a narrow-eyed glance. He had changed, his hair was still damp from the shower, but instead of the lounge suit which he usually wore when dining at home, he was wearing a superbly cut evening jacket.

'Are you going out?' Mrs Hurst enquired.

'Yes,' he answered his mother briefly, his eyes still on Gina. 'Gina and I are going to a reception later. I'm taking her back to Town with me.'

'She never said anything.'

'Because she didn't know.' Quentin, as though impatient of his mother's hurt surprise, was curt.

Gina was startled and knew her face betrayed it. She hadn't appeared anywhere with Quentin, apart from their wedding reception, and their one trip to London which could scarcely have been called a social occasion. This evening she felt ill equipped to make her debut, if that was what he intended.

'Do you really mean it?' she asked.

'Yes.' He remained uncompromising, meeting Gina's wide eyes with cool belligerence. 'And before you begin attacking me for not giving you a ring, I did try, but you weren't in, and I didn't feel like leaving a message.'

'I went to see my grandfather,' she faltered, growing cold as this reminded her how Quentin must have saved Charles from heartache and possible disgrace. Knowing this, how could she oppose him in anything, ever again? With the meekness which she saw continued to surprise him, she added hesitantly, 'He rang and asked me over. They've only just got home, but I'm sorry I wasn't here when you wanted me.'

His brows rose, while his eyes lost none of their cynical intentness. 'You'll come this evening, then?'

He was asking, she realised, if she intended coming quietly. Did she really have a choice? 'Yes, if you still want me.' She was astonished at the steadiness of her voice when she was a quiver of nerves inside. She noticed he didn't answer her oddly worded query. Perhaps he didn't want her any more? She could scarcely expect him to.

'Wear one of your Paris dresses,' was all he said, as they went in to dinner.

'Is it something special?' Mrs Hurst asked as they sat down.

'In a way,' Quentin nodded his handsome head. 'A lot of people are getting very curious about my wife,' he addressed his mother as if Gina wasn't there. 'I'll have to produce her sooner or later and this evening seems as good a time as any. One or two important clients are on the guest list and I more or less promised I'd turn up.'

If he had loved her, Gina would have been full of pleasure and excitement at the prospect of such an occasion. But Quentin didn't love her and she was too aware of the weight of her own troubled conscience to be able to relax. For all this, she knew she had never looked lovelier than she did, when she came downstairs to find him waiting for her in the hall.

'Quite entrancingly beautiful, but absurdly young,' he said tightly, almost as if her youthfulness annoyed him.

'Nothing that time won't alter, sir,' Matthews, allowing himself the privilege of an old and trusted servant, smiled at Gina indulgently. Gallantly he added, 'You're looking very lovely, Mrs Quentin, but I doubt that time will alter that.'

Gina smiled at him warmly, yet a little sadly as she said goodbye. If only she had been a little older and wiser she might have been so happy here. Matthews and the rest of the staff were so nice to her now, and she might soon have to leave it all behind.

Her heart heavy, she followed Quentin outside. Should she speak to him on the way to London? He didn't usually talk much when he was driving, but she suddenly felt she couldn't wait.

Having expected Quentin to be driving himself, she

was surprised to find Hardy, his man from London, behind the wheel. 'Hardy's driving,' Quentin explained, briefly. 'It's not so tiring. We'll stay in Town tonight and he can take you home in the morning.'

'What about my horses?'

'Oh, my God!' he murmured sarcastically, his eyes hardening at Gina's quick consternation. 'Your horses! Sometimes I wish I had four legs! The gardener will see to them, he's done it before. I had a word with him, and also my mother, while you were upstairs.'

'I see . . .' Gina wasn't sure that she felt happy about the arrangement, but the gleam in Quentin's eyes advised her against arguing. She wasn't sure about staying in Town, either, but again she decided against saying anything. Quentin was in a strange mood and she didn't want to antagonise him further.

She didn't get a chance to mention her grandfather's money, and how mistaken she had been about it as he soon squashed any hopes she had had of a cosy chat in the back of the car. Quentin sat in front with Hardy and only spoke to her occasionally over his shoulder.

The party, given by an overseas consortium, was well under way by the time they arrived, and she felt grateful that she had attended several such functions with Charles and Liza during the year she had lived with them. Otherwise she might have felt rather overwhelmed. All she could see were crowds of people and her ears were immediately assaulted by an ever-increasing volume of conversation and laughter. There was dancing, but the music for this merely seemed to add to the general noise.

'Come on,' Quentin drew her forward grimly, 'you're young, don't forget. A little of this goes a long way but won't hurt you.'

Because this sounded too much like criticism, her raw nerves wouldn't stand for it and she protested jerkily, 'I've scarcely got through the door!'

'And already attracting attention.' He seemed no more

pleased about this, but abruptly, as they were hailed by a
nearby group, he said, 'Come and meet some of my
friends.'

As Charles Hearn's newly discovered granddaughter,
Gina had captured quite a lot of interest at the parties she
had gone to with him, but this was slightly different, she
discovered, from the interest these people displayed in
Quentin's wife. There was general surprise, she sensed, at
her youth, but while the men regarded her with open
admiration some of the women were frankly envious. The
year she had travelled abroad had given her confidence
and a little sophistication which was altogether attractive,
but she realised these female friends of Quentin's might
have welcomed her better if she had been older and
plain.

Mostly, throughout the evening, she didn't stray far
from Quentin's side, but plenty of men clamoured to talk
and dance with her and she found it difficult to refuse
them. Quentin encouraged her, and appeared to enjoy an
occasional change of partner himself, but his eyes seldom
left Gina for long. One woman in particular followed him
around, casting him languishing glances and contriving
to ignore his wife. When one of the men who bore Gina
off to dance murmured tipsily in her ear that Margot
Jones was an old girl-friend of Quentin's, she wasn't surprised to hear it.

After this, although she refused to believe she could be
jealous, Gina found it difficult to even pretend to be enjoying herself, and it must have showed, because Quentin
rebuked her again.

'I know you aren't enchanted with me, darling,' he
drawled sardonically, 'but you could make an effort. A
few smiles wouldn't come amiss. They're what's expected
of a bride.'

'Is it important?' she asked, more bitterly than she realised.

'For my pride's sake, I think it is.' He held her cruelly close as they circled the crowded floor, his eyes cynical.

'I'm sorry,' she said, adding truthfully, 'I'm not in a party mood this evening.'

'Are you ever?' he snapped, suddenly angry.

In view of her own aching unhappiness, this was too much. Impulsively she retorted, 'I'm sure no one's giving us that much attention, except, perhaps, Miss Jones!'

'Jealous?'

'I—I might be,' she admitted, trembling, suddenly too mixed up to be anything else but completely honest.

Quentin laughed tauntingly. 'How much have you had to drink? I noticed your last partner was keeping you well supplied.'

'Only one or two,' she said stiffly.

'Altogether?'

She tried to remember. 'That's all, apart from the Martini you got me.'

He frowned, but the music stopped before he could comment and Margot Jones just happened to be there. Quite without shame she curled her hands around Quentin's arm as he released Gina.

'You were married in an awful hurry, weren't you, darling?' she purred, her eyes running maliciously down the length of Gina's slender figure.

Gina boiled. 'I wasn't pregnant, if that's what you mean? Not that it would have mattered,' she faltered, her rush of resentment dwindling unhappily into embarrassment. How could she have come out with that, especially as she hadn't even slept with Quentin yet!

His sideways glance mockingly asked the same question, and it seemed to her his revenge was complete—equally divided between Margot and herself, when he drawled smoothly, 'But you soon could be.'

While Gina went white and Margot flushed with temper, he appeared quite unrepentant. Yet Gina noticed he was slightly puzzled by the momentary unhappiness she had betrayed. Miss Jones was angry. It was so obvious there could be no doubt, and Gina was relieved when some other friends of Quentin's arrived, for she had no wish to be part of an ugly scene.

Had Margot Jones been Quentin's mistress? If she had been, Gina felt sorry for her, for he seemed to regard her now with callous indifference. As he would herself, Gina had no illusions, after she made her confession, later.

It was almost two in the morning before Quentin decided they would leave, and even then he didn't appear in any great hurry to return to the flat.

'Would you like some supper?' he enquired, as they went out to their taxi.

'Supper?'

'It's not impossible,' he assured her dryly.

'It's not that.' She had been trying to decide how best to make her apologies, for her guilty, aching conscience wouldn't allow her to put off any longer. Supper, she felt, would choke her. It might, of course, be easier to stay out until dawn when Quentin would just have time to shower and change before going to the office, but this would only mean postponement, and she had surely done enough of that already.

'What is it, then?' Quentin persisted tersely.

'I'd rather go straight back to the flat.'

'Well, don't look so anguished,' he said curtly. 'Nothing's going to happen.'

Something might, but not perhaps what he imagined!

'I didn't imagine anything would.' She contrived to speak lightly.

As her voice came over more carelessly than she intended, he bit out savagely, 'I expect you think I wouldn't have the nerve to follow up what I said to Margot Jones?'

'That was as much my fault as yours.' She spoke huskily, her heart racing. Dear God, why couldn't he

shut up? What devious delight did he derive from taunting her so?

'Hmm,' he turned his head slightly to consider her
thoughtfully, 'why did you come out with that, Gina?
You said earlier you weren't jealous.'

'Well . . .' she stammered, beginning to realise she
could be on dangerous ground.

'Sooner or later,' he drawled conversationally, 'it may
come to that, you know. Either that, or we part for good.'

Gina was trembling on both counts, and he probably
knew it. Was he trying to force the responsibility of such a
decision on her? Had seeing Margot Jones made him
regret his hasty marriage, which wasn't really a marriage
at all? Well, the confession she was shortly to make might
bring things to a head. She had rejected him unfairly,
and in return he had rejected her, and never in all the
weeks of their marriage had he given any serious indication of changing his mind. Now she suspected he was
trying to force her into a corner, from which he probably
hoped she would flee, never to return again!

Such dramatic thoughts played havoc with Gina's abi-
lity to think straight. All she could whisper was, 'I have
to talk to you, but not here.'

She was mortified that Quentin merely looked bored.
'I think we're both too tired. Leave it until I get home
tonight.'

'Tonight? Oh, I see. It's already a new day.'

'A new day?' He appeared to be pondering over that,
because he laughed, turning away from her cynically. 'Is
it? Who would have guessed?'

He didn't mention supper again but took her straight
back to the apartment.

'Where's Hardy?' she whispered.

'He has his own quarters, in the basement,' Quentin
shrugged, as they went upstairs.

Gina shivered, not because of this but because she was
trying to decide where to begin. She couldn't leave it!

'You made quite an impression tonight.' As if sensing the tension in her and seeking to relieve it with a little light teasing, he smiled. 'I shall have to watch you in future.'

In future? Did he really mean them to have one—together? Hope swept through her, briefly dispersing some of the unhappiness from her face. Anxiously she turned to him. Perhaps if she explained carefully he would be tolerant? 'Quentin——?' she began.

'No, Gina.' Silencing her abruptly, he held up his hand, 'Haven't I told you, no more tonight. I think you'd be better in bed.'

Painfully she bit her lip. Maybe he was right. She had tried, but he wouldn't listen. It might be a better idea to wait, after all, for no matter what she said he seemed determined to forestall her. Wearily she nodded her shining head, then found herself smiling ruefully as something occurred to her. 'I've just remembered, I've brought nothing to sleep in. You'll have to loan me a pair of pyjamas.'

'That's my fault.' He seemed relieved that she was being sensible. 'I rushed you away from Briarly without mentioning that you'd be staying here, but you're certainly welcome to my pyjamas, if they'll do.'

'Yes,' she said, 'they'll be fine.'

'Just as long as you don't get lost in them,' he grinned, eyeing her much smaller proportions.

'No, I won't,' she said hastily. 'Could you leave them on my bed while I wash, please?'

Quentin didn't say anything, but when she finished in the bathroom she found them placed neatly on her pillow. They were, as he had suggested, much too big for her, but she rolled up the legs and sleeves. At least they covered every bit of her.

Before she got into bed, feeling the beginnings of a head-ache coming on, she decided to go down to the kitchen for some aspirin. There was none that she could discover in the bathroom, but she couldn't find any in the kitchen, either. So there was nothing for it but to ask Quentin. Her head was so very muzzy from the wine she had drunk that if she didn't get something she mightn't be able to get out of bed in the morning. Then what would Hardy think!

It must be rather unusual, she thought, for a wife not to know where her husband slept. Uncertainly she knocked on the door next to her own, but on receiving no answer made her way to the next. It was then that disaster overtook her. One of the rolled up legs of Quentin's pyjamas fell down, tripping her up and bringing her crashing down on to the carpet that covered the corridor.

She didn't think she had made a lot of noise, but it was sufficient to bring Quentin running. She was struggling to her feet by the time he got there, and was indignant that he had the effrontery to laugh as she tried to extricate herself from what seemed like miles of green silk pyjamas and the heavy, tumbling mass of her long red hair.

Instantly, seeing her distress, he placed his hands on her shaking shoulders to steady her. 'What on earth were you trying to do?' he asked, his laughter fading grimly.

Gina gulped, endeavouring to find breath to explain about the aspirin, when everything seemed to die in her throat. Without quite realising what was happening, she found herself clinging to him, her arms going wildly around him. 'Quentin,' she whispered helplessly, her face buried against his bare chest, tears streaming unchecked down her hot cheeks.

He stiffened, then caught her tightly to him, savagely uttering a smothered oath as he pulled her fiercely into his arms. He didn't speak, he appeared to decide words weren't necessary as he swept her up and strode with her into his room, sharply closing the door. It was as if something inside him had given way before primitive forces he could no longer control. There was only the harsh rasp of his breathing as he laid her on the bed and came down beside her.

Gina's senses reeled. Again she tried to speak, but nothing came. She felt dizzy, her eyes dazed and she knew she was slowly breaking. All of a sudden she didn't care any more. Why go on fighting him, torturing herself? After he knew the truth he might never want her again.

He did now. Not even her innocence could hide from her the urgency in the hard body crushing hers. Blindly she turned her head to press trembling lips against his cheek, as he bent to kiss her throat.

'Gina,' he groaned, all the anger and coldness of the last weeks leaving him, his voice warm with desire.

His mouth moved over her bare shoulders, back to her face, as naked they clung together. She wasn't sure what had happened to the green silk pyjamas, but they suddenly weren't there any more. Neither were his.

'Gina,' he groaned again, his mouth moving over her lips, 'how I've wanted you! All the time—beyond endurance . . .'

He muttered more, as he parted her lips passionately, but her ringing ears prevented her from hearing much of what he said. Her limbs were invaded by a curious lethargy as his kisses became deeper and hungrier, more intimately demanding, and she could only cling to him, feeling herself growing weaker and more helpless.

She shuddered as his hands teased the rosy peaks of her taut breasts, until she was overwhelmingly aware that this wasn't enough. She had to be closer. No longer could she deny herself the satisfaction of belonging to him completely.

'Love me, Quentin,' she moaned, 'please love me.' Nothing else seemed to matter.

She didn't have to ask him twice. With urgent insistence his mouth crushed hers, and soon he had her bones turning to water, as he caressed her until she melted against him, making her need as great as his own. Then, as though he knew the exact moment, his hands were curving under her hips and the full weight of his body was no longer to be escaped, or denied her.

There was pain, but this almost immediately dissolved in incredible pleasure, her first frightened cry being lost against his lips and soon forgotten. It was like a battle. They had wanted each other for so long, but they couldn't have guessed the potency of the final outcome. The strength of the waves of burning passion which swept them wildly into realms of rapture which not even Quentin, with his greater experience, had ever known before.

Afterwards, Gina was so tired she fell asleep almost at once, with Quentin's arms still around her, holding her tightly, as if she were something very precious. She was drowsy when she woke with the first light, to find him propped on an elbow, staring down at her.

Sleepily she smiled at him, conscious of nothing in that first moment of awakening but a sense of well-being. At first it didn't seem odd that he didn't smile back. She wasn't immediately worried. It seemed enough that they were together.

But as his stare grew prolonged and he still didn't speak, she lifted a shy hand to tentatively touch his face. 'Darling?' she murmured eagerly, very aware now of what had happened between them.

He tensed at the touch of her fingers on his skin, but his eyes were still hard as he asked derisively. 'Well? And how do you feel this morning, Gina, now that you're really the wife of a thief?'

So that was what was wrong? Shocked, she shrank away from him, and, as memory flooded back, she cried, 'You don't understand, Quentin. I know you aren't a—a thief. Grandfather told me yesterday.'

'Your grandfather?'

'Yes . . .' She was very muddled and distracted. Words began tumbling out the wrong way because she didn't want to talk. All she wanted was for Quentin to make love to her again. She wanted to put her arms around him, to rub her cheek against his. To have him kiss her and hold her close, until she could scarcely breathe—or think. 'It just came out by mistake, I suppose.'

'So you decided to make sure of me?'

'Make sure of you?' she croaked.

'You don't have to sound so bewildered, darling.' His heavy sarcasm came over quite clearly, widening her eyes with apprehension. 'You didn't want to be the wife of a poor man, who took money from defenceless old men, but you didn't mind belonging to a rich one.'

'No, Quentin,' suddenly she began to realise what he was getting at, 'it wasn't the money. At least,' she tried to be honest, 'it wasn't so much that I thought you'd taken it from Grandfather, it was more that you seemed to be making no effort to pay it back.'

He ignored that. 'You didn't trust me.'

'No,' Gina agreed dully, her face bleak as she suddenly realised the weight of evidence against her, 'No, I suppose I didn't. Someone told me, a few days before we were married, that you'd lost all your money and had borrowed from my grandfather, and I believed them,' she whispered, shamefaced.

'Yet you went ahead and married me?'

'I was going to do that, anyway.'

'Why?' he snapped savagely.

She shook her head hopelessly. She couldn't tell him one of the reasons had been she loved him, not when he had never said he loved her. 'I'm not sure,' she replied evasively. 'I believe I had some foolish ideas about revenge. I remembered how you used to say I was untidy, and treated me as though I was just a foolish child. That sort of thing, you know.'

'Yes, I know,' he said grimly, 'but I was convinced you were beginning to forget.'

'I was,' she confessed bitterly, 'until this other came up. It seemed to bring it all back.'

'And the money was what was really behind your refusal to consummate our marriage? Why you insisted on having only a short honeymoon in Vienna?'

Unhappily she nodded, tears gathering in her eyes even to think of it. 'I'm sorry, Quentin.'

'Not half as sorry as I was.' His mouth went tight as he watched her cheeks grow pink under her tears. 'Have you any idea how I suffered?'

Swallowing hard, she whispered again, 'I'm sorry. I did try to tell you, last night, that I knew it was Grandfather who'd borrowed money from you, but you wouldn't listen.'

'You couldn't have tried very hard,' he observed cuttingly. 'I don't suppose it occurred to you that without my support you and your grandfather would be penniless? Obviously you decided to make sure I couldn't get rid of you so easily.'

'No!' She felt flayed by his vindictive tones and beyond everything but the truth. 'I love you, Quentin. When you began making love to me I forgot everything else.'

Clearly he didn't believe her, because he made no reply. Instead, he left the bed and reached for his dressing gown. 'Hardy will take you home,' he said, watching cynically as she struggled to cover herself with the sheet he had thrown aside. 'I'll see you this evening, when we can discuss what we're going to do. A separation might be better for both of us, I'm only sorry it can't now be an annulment. Don't worry, though, you won't lose out, whatever you choose. I'll see you have more than enough to live on, although you certainly won't be living with me.'

Gina must have lain stunned for almost an hour after he left. He didn't return and she was quite convinced he meant every word he said.

At nine she rose, feeling terribly shaken but knowing she couldn't go back to Briarly yet. Mrs Hurst would only need to glance at her to see something was wrong, and she would hate that. She had only her evening dress, but because it was made of fine material she was able to hitch it up over a belt, under her fur coat. Her gold slippers looked slightly ridiculous, but they would have to do. No one would notice, and what did it matter if they did? Leaving a note for Hardy in the hall, to say she wouldn't need him, she slipped out unobserved.

She was never sure exactly where she walked that day, or how far. For hours she wandered around the shops, staring sightlessly in windows, and when she grew cold she went inside. It was late October and people were beginning their Christmas shopping and the stores were busy. No one looked twice at a small, redheaded girl with a haunted expression. At lunch time she discovered she had enough for a cup of coffee and afterwards she went to a park and sat staring at nothing in particular. She didn't notice when it began to rain, or that she was getting wetter by the minute. The rain streaming down her face merely mixed with the tears. She couldn't even think about Quentin. When she did there was so much pain she couldn't bear it. Her life was ruined because of her own foolishness—she had no one but herself to blame.

It was late, and dark, when she realised she couldn't stay out all night. Already a couple of men had given her suggestive glances which had penetrated even her thick fog of unhappiness and frightened her, Reluctantly she decided to go back to the flat. Quentin would be at Briarly and she had nothing to fear from Hardy. He was too well trained to ask questions.

Ringing the doorbell with fingers so numb she could scarcely press it, she was startled by the speed with which the door opened. To her amazement and dismay Quentin stood there.

'Gina!' his dark face was distraught. 'Oh, my God.

Thank God!' she heard him breathing repeatedly, as she fainted dead away. 'Thank God you've come back!'

When she came round she was lying on the big sofa in the lounge, wrapped in rugs, with Quentin bending over her, moistening her lips with brandy and rubbing her hands. Hardy was hovering just as anxiously in the background, but when she opened her eyes he was quickly dismissed.

'Oh, Gina,' Quentin groaned, for seconds appearing almost too moved to speak, 'are you feeling better? I've been worried sick—you've given us a terrible fright!'

Uncertainly Gina blinked, scrubbing a weak tear from her eye. She felt all right. The frightening numbness was going, dispelled by the warmth of the room. Her glance wandered to Quentin's face and she saw how pale he was. She would have expected him to look angry instead of full of remorse.

'I'm sorry, Quentin,' she bent her head, 'I didn't mean to alarm anyone but I was so miserable I had to get away. I just walked and walked.'

'And I've searched and searched!' As though recalling every minute of it, his face contorted grimly. 'You weren't at Briarly, or with your grandfather. You weren't here. I even checked with the police. I've had to ring them and report you've been found.'

Startled, Gina asked, 'Have you been looking long? I wish I'd known . . .'

'Since ten this morning,' he replied harshly, his grip tightening on her slender hands. 'That was when I realised I couldn't do without you, but you weren't here and I've gone through the tortures of hell trying to find you.'

'It wasn't your fault,' she said huskily, 'I ought to have trusted you, as I said before.'

'No,' he hushed her bleakly, 'I can understand now how you felt, now I've had time to think it over. This morning I was too full of stiff pride, just as I was when you rejected me on our honeymoon. You were young and unsure, and if I'd been more understanding I would have had more patience. I'd have taken time to discover what was troubling you—and I knew something was. I should have explained about the money and told you that I loved you instead of letting you wonder why I'd married you, and things deteriorate between us.'

'You love me?' Her voice croaked with incredulity while she closed her eyes against another storm of quick tears. It didn't seem possible!

'Gina?' Anxiously he put a gentle arm around her, 'Of course I love you, but you can't be feeling well enough to talk. Later perhaps,' grimly he smoothed back her damp hair. 'I think, right now, I should be sending for a doctor.'

'No,' she shook her head, quickly and truthfully, 'I'm feeling fine, honestly I am! If you'll just tell me when you began loving me, it will do me more good than anything else.'

Bending his dark head, he gently kissed her soft lips. 'I've been fond of you all your life, but I didn't suspect it was more than a mild affection until I had you in my arms, by the lake. Even then I didn't recognise it for what it was, not until I heard your father had died.'

'My father?'

'Yes,' he replied soberly. 'When my mother rang me in Australia and mentioned it, I couldn't think of anyone but you. I just dropped everything and came home, which caused quite a few raised eyebrows, I can tell you, but somehow I couldn't bear to think of you being all alone at a time like that. It was then that I realised I loved you and wanted to look after you.'

With a grim half smile, his lips twisted as he met her widening eyes. 'I had only to see you again, of course, to be convinced I'd made a mistake. You were so young and antagonistic, and quite clearly you didn't love me. I suspected I could probably make you care for me, but it seemed suddenly inconceivable that you could make me a suitable wife. Oh, my darling,' he groaned against her cheek, 'if you've doubted me, I've been no better. I didn't feel I could trust you not to wreak havoc in my life. As you stood there, so small and untidy, defying me, I felt suddenly, terribly angry. I decided the only sensible thing to do was to get rid of you—but remember you fainted? I knew, as I carried you upstairs that night and sat by your bedside, that I couldn't send you away. But I hoped that the fire, the consuming need I felt for you, would soon burn itself out. I tried ignoring you, I even used Blanche Edgar as a sort of wedge between us, but it still didn't work.'

'I thought you were going to marry her,' Gina whispered.

'No, never,' he assured her, adding wryly, 'If I ever hinted, or gave you any other indication that I might care for her, it was only to make you jealous.'

'You said you were trying to put me off?' Gina frowned.

'That, too,' Quentin's brows rose derisively. 'I guess for a man who's always known his own mind, you had me pretty mixed up.'

'You should have sent me away,' she sighed remorsefully, only beginning to understand the trouble she had caused him.

He caught the hand she pressed to his face and kissed it sensuously. 'I couldn't. I'd planned to buy you and your father a house in the village, but when he died I couldn't tolerate the idea of your living alone. I was almost at the end of my tether, though, with wanting you, when Charles told me he believed you were his granddaughter. Then I was devastated! When your grandfather mentioned the time I'd spent proving you really were his granddaughter, he was wrong. I'd actually been trying to prove you were not, because I couldn't bear to part with you. The night I kissed you in the stables revealed to me the depth of my own feelings too clearly. But you were such a babe, you'd seen nothing of the world—or men—so how could I possibly keep you? I had to let you go, to spread your wings a little, give you time to grow up and know your own mind. During the year you were away I never completely lost sight of you, but it was the worst year I've ever spent. When you came home—I like to think, back to me, so beautiful and more assured—I had to have you. From then on I was determined!'

Quentin had done most of the talking, but when he paused Gina believed she was the more breathless. 'You never said you loved me.'

'I thought you didn't love me, and I seemed to have betrayed myself a hundred times over—always ringing you, asking you out, not being able to take my eyes off you.' He paused, his face pale as he stared at her. 'I helped Charles, when he was in financial difficulties, chiefly because I loved you. When he begged me not to mention this, I agreed, but again because I was thinking more of myself, I'm afraid. I didn't want you marrying me out of gratitude, but I did think you were beginning to love me, until our infamous trip to Vienna.'

'Oh, darling,' she murmured, contrite tears in her eyes, her heartbeats unsteady, 'I did love you. I wasn't just beginning to, but I thought you'd married me for my grandfather's money, after what . . .'

'After what Blanche told you,' Quentin's voice was harsh as Gina hesitated. 'Most of which she made up, I imagine, from one or two rumours she had heard in the City. She certainly got nothing from me. Charles mentioned what she'd said, this afternoon.'

'I asked him not to.'

'Well, he did. He was as worried as I was.'

'Yes, I see.' Uncertainly she glanced at him. 'I'd better let him know nothing's happened to me.'

'Hardy's already done that.' He gathered her closer to him. 'We'll go and see him tomorrow, before we set off on a proper honeymoon.'

'Quentin!' she protested, her cheeks flushing, her limbs trembling as he suddenly picked her up, rug and all, in his arms. 'Where are you taking me?'

'You mean for a honeymoon or now?' he teased gently.

'Now—well, both, I suppose,' she stammered, though his immediate plans became very apparent as he strode with her from the room.

'I love you,' he replied thickly, his face darkening, as if that should supply the answer.

As he laid her on his bed and began kissing her, her pulse began racing. 'Quentin,' she pleaded, her breathing quickening with his, 'when you proposed to me at the cottage, you did it so abruptly. I couldn't believe you loved me.'

His mouth, so near her own, went taut with remembered pain. 'I wanted to give you time, but I found I couldn't wait—perhaps that was why I sounded so abrupt. It was all I could do to get myself out of there without making you completely mine. Didn't you guess?'

Silently Gina shook her head. 'No, but I might have done, now. I mean,' the confusion in her eyes deepened adorably, as she bravely met his, 'after last night.'

Lowering his head, Quentin kissed her very gently, then crushed her fiercely to him, neither his arms or mouth so gentle any more. Gruffly, against her lips he murmured, 'Did you mind, darling, about last night?'

'Only some of the things you said afterwards, but I'll forgive you if . . .'

'If what?'

'If,' her eager arms curled around his neck possessively, 'if I don't always have to trip over in corridors in order to get into your bed!'

He laughed and her bright smile flickered, before their teasing glances sobered almost instantly as passion took over.

'Darling, my small torment, I love you,' he groaned, his mouth ardent on her lips, his hands on her body.

'And I you,' she trembled, trying to control the waves of sensuous desire he was deliberately arousing and which were rapidly overpowering her. Breathlessly she managed to gasp, 'Didn't Hardy say something about dinner? Won't he be waiting?'

'Let him wait,' Quentin replied, taking her mouth again with passionate indifference.

And Hardy had to.

We value your opinion. . .

You can help us make our books even better by completing and mailing this questionnaire. Please check [✓] the appropriate boxes.

1. Compared to romance series by other publishers, do Harlequin novels have any additional features that make them more attractive?

   1.1 ☐ yes   .2 ☐ no   .3 ☐ don't know

   If yes, what additional features? _____

   _____

   _____

2. How much do these additional features influence your purchasing of Harlequin novels?

   2.1 ☐ a great deal   .2 ☐ somewhat   .3 ☐ not at all   .4 ☐ not sure

3. Are there any other additional features you would like to include?

   _____

   _____

   _____

4. Where did you obtain this book?

   4.1 ☐ bookstore   .4 ☐ borrowed or traded

   .2 ☐ supermarket   .5 ☐ subscription

   .3 ☐ other store   .6 ☐ other (please specify)_____

5. How long have you been reading Harlequin novels?

   5.1 ☐ less than 3 months   .4 ☐ 1-3 years

   .2 ☐ 3-6 months   .5 ☐ more than 3 years

   .3 ☐ 7-11 months   .6 ☐ don't remember

6. Please indicate your age group.

   6.1 ☐ younger than 18   .3 ☐ 25-34   .5 ☐ 50 or older

   .2 ☐ 18-24   .4 ☐ 35-49

Please mail to: **Harlequin Reader Service**

In U.S.A.	In Canada
1440 South Priest Drive	649 Ontario Street
Tempe, AZ 85281	Stratford, Ontario N5A 6W2

Thank you very much for your cooperation.